NINA JAFFE

PATAKÍN

World Tales of
Drums and Drummers

with drawings by
ELLEN EAGLE

HENRY HOLT AND COMPANY • NEW YORK

Henry Holt and Company, Inc. / *Publishers since 1866*
115 West 18th Street / New York, New York 10011

Henry Holt is a registered trademark of Henry Holt and Company, Inc.

Copyright © 1994 by Nina Jaffe
All rights reserved.
Published in Canada by Fitzhenry & Whiteside Ltd.,
195 Allstate Parkway, Markham, Ontario L3R 4T8.

Library of Congress Cataloging-in-Publication Data
Jaffe, Nina.
Patakin: world tales of drums and drummers / by Nina Jaffe.
Includes bibliographical references.
1. Drum—Folklore.   2. Tales.   [1. Drum—Folklore.   2. Folklore.]
GR885.4.J341994   398.27—dc20   93-42790

ISBN 0-8050-3005-0 / First Edition—1994

The author is grateful to the following: Father Jack Johnson and the Oblate Provincial House in Edmonton, Alberta, Canada, for permission to retell (as "Skeleton Woman") the Inuit story "The Magic Drum," which appears in *Tales from the Igloo* by Father Maurice Metayer (Edmonton, Alberta: Hurtig Publishers, Ltd., 1972); Stemmer House, for permission to retell "The Drum That Lost Its Voice," which appears in the collection *Tales from the South Pacific* by Ann Gittins (Owings Mills, MD: Stemmer House, 1977); Charles E. Tuttle Publishing Co., Inc., for permission to retell (as "Hyuk-San and the Tiger") the story "The Father's Legacy," which appears in *The Story Bag: A Collection of Korean Folktales* by Kim So-Un (Rutland, VT: Charles E. Tuttle Publishing Co., Inc., 1955); The University of California at Los Angeles Latin American Center, for permission to retell (as "Neima's Rescue") portions of "Neima and the Evil Spirits," which is included in volume 2 of *Folk Literature of the Guajiro Indians*, edited by Johannes Wilbert and Karen Simoneau (Los Angeles: University of California at Los Angeles Latin American Center Publications, 1986).

Many thanks to Professor Harold Courlander, for permission to retell the story "The Elephant King's Drum," which was first published in his collection *The Piece of Fire and Other Haitian Tales* (New York: Harcourt, Brace and World, 1964) under the title "Merisier, Stronger Than the Elephants," and for permission to retell the story "Anansi and the Secret Name," which appears in his book *The King's Drum and Other African Stories* (New York: Harcourt, Brace and World, 1962) under the title "Sky God's Daughter."

Permission for the following music notations is gratefully acknowledged: David MacAllester and Royal Hartigan, p. 5; Royal Hartigan and Richard Hill, p. 13; Abraham Kobena Adzenyah and Royal Hartigan, pp. 27, 28; Royal Hartigan, pp. 39, 40, 78, 112, 113; Sang Won Park (song transcribed by Mrs. Cho Tai Sun), p. 60; Ramnad Raghavan, p. 67; Francisco Dominguez, p. 103.

Printed in the United States of America on acid-free paper. ∞
10 9 8 7 6 5 4 3 2 1

To the memory of Ken Feit,
storyteller, spirit traveler,
who long ago on a windy
street corner in Minneapolis
encouraged me to tell the
myth of the drum.

El tambor, el tambor,
El tambor de la alegría.
Yo quiero que tu me lleves
Al tambor de la alegría.

The drum, the drum,
The drum of happiness.
Bring me to
The drum of happiness.

—A Panamanian folk song

Acknowledgments

♫ ♫ ♫

The gathering and writing of these stories would not have been possible without the help and generosity of scholars, ethnomusicologists, and musicians who in their professional lives have devoted themselves to the recording, documentation, and performance of world musical traditions. For sharing sources and important cultural background I am indebted to John Bierhorst and Harold Courlander; to the Alaska Native Languages Center at the University of Alaska at Fairbanks; to Gage Averill, John Kelsey, and the staff of the World Music Archives at Wesleyan University in Middletown, Connecticut; and to Richard Hill, Kate Kinney, Eun Kyung Kwon, Mick Maloney, Morty Marks, Dr. Israel Ross, Mei Mei Sanford, and Sam Solberg. Also to staff members of the Fiji Mission to the United Nations, the World Music Institute, the Korean Cultural Service, and the Library for Performing Arts at Lincoln Center. I am grateful to Royal Hartigan (San Jose State University and the New School for Social Research) for reviewing the text and illustrations and for contributing notations and important commentary. Special thanks are also due to musicians Frisner Augustin, Christy Barry, Paul Leake, Sabah Nissan, Sang Won Park, and Adeleke Sangogoyin, who in so generously sharing their knowledge and experiences inspired or gave substance to several stories in the book; and to Steve Gorn, Victor Jaroslaw, David MacAllester, Bill Ochs, Alice Olwell, David Reck, Judith Cook Tucker, and Glen Velez.

My editor, Marc Aronson, is owed many thanks for his creative insights, attention to detail, and expert guidance throughout the shaping of the book, as is Andy Packer for untold hours of editorial assistance and moral support.

My deepest thanks to the musicians who taught me the discipline as well as joy of playing the drums of their traditions: Abraham Kobena Adzenyah and Ramnad Raghavan of Wesleyan University's World Music Program and Louis Bauzo, director of the Latin Music Program at the Harbor Performing Arts Center in New York City; to two inspiring teachers of creative movement—the late Mara Capy and the late Katya Delakova—both of whom had profound influence on my work in storytelling; and to my mother, Grace Carol Jaffe, a Dalcroze Eurhythmics teacher, who raised me with dance, music, and cross-rhythms.

Most of all, I wish to thank my husband, Bob, for his patience and support, and my son, Louis, who listened to the stories as they emerged and who once said, "When there's thunder, it means that God is playing Shiva's drum."

Contents

☙ ☙ ☙

Introduction

ⵉ ⵉ ⵉ

atakín (pronounced "pah-tah-*keen*") is a word from Afro-Cuban culture that means "story" or "legend." When Spain controlled Cuba, many African slaves were brought to the island from the Yoruba Empire in what is now southwestern Nigeria. Soon Yoruba language, custom, and traditions were incorporated into the evolving Cuban culture. *Patakín* is one of those words. The traditional religion of the Yoruba is centered on the worship of gods and goddesses called *orisha* (oh-*ree*-shah). A person who is in need of help or advice will go to the priest, known as a *babalao* (bah-bah-*lah*-oh), to seek counsel. Using ancient techniques of divination, the priest will throw down a number of objects such as cowrie shells or palm nuts and observe the patterns they fall into. Each pattern corresponds to a set of verses and a story about one of the gods or goddesses, which the priest will use to instruct the person. *Patakín* refers to these tales of the orisha, studied and learned over many years, that have wisdom to impart or lessons to teach.

To my drummer's ear, the word also sounds like the low, middle, and high tones of the conga drum—"pa-ta-kín." Perhaps this is as it should be, since every drum has its own language, its own tones and phrases. It is the drummer, through his or her training and skill, who learns how to speak and play that special language. From Africa to Asia, from Europe to North America to the Pacific Islands, every drum has a story to tell, and every drummer has his or her own way of "saying" and playing it.

This book will introduce you to drums and drummers from around the world. Drums are among the most sacred, the most ancient, of all musical instruments. Since early times, the power of drums and rhythms has been well known and respected in many cultures. There is a Hebrew saying dating from the first century that goes, "From six to sixty, she becomes nimble at the sound of the timbrel." (A timbrel is a small hand drum, like a tambourine.) In ancient Palestine, drums were played at religious festivals, as well as at weddings and celebrations. Among the Bayankole in East Africa there was even a special house built for the drums of the village. There the drums were carefully kept, and they were removed only for ceremonial occasions. Gods and goddesses from many cultures have been credited with bringing drums into the world. But drumming is also a natural part of everyday life. After all, drumming rhythms reflect the steady beat of the heart, the natural cadences of running and walking, of work and play. You can even see little babies "drum for joy" on pots and pans when they just want to make some noise. Whether you are banging a stick on a can or practicing on a drum set, the desire and ability to make rhythms come alive are part of every child, every human being. One of my drumming teachers, Abraham Kobena Adzenyah, a Ghanaian master drummer, used to say, "The music is for sharing. Even if you just clap your hands, you are part of it." In Ghana, music and drumming are considered the birthright of every member of the community.

In societies throughout the world, both women and men have participated in music-making: dancing, singing, composing, and playing instruments. According to the practices and beliefs of each culture, their roles have shifted and changed over time. Today you can see women and men, boys and girls, playing percussion instruments in rock, jazz, and salsa bands and even in classical music ensembles. In this book, the characters who drum are male or female (or even animal!) according to the way the stories were handed down in the traditions from which they originated. Of course, the very purpose of *Patakín* is to invite everyone to participate in these rhythms and forms of musical expression.

The stories in this book will take you into some

new and different worlds where drums can be used to conquer demons, bring a skeleton back to life, or tame a fearful tiger. Each drum has its own set of tones and rhythms, some of which will be shown to you in the introduction to the stories. In many cultures worldwide, the drumming patterns have been passed down orally, from teacher to students, or within families, without the use of written notation. When needed, I have included Western notation as a "translation" of the oral patterns. If you don't know how to read music, ask a teacher or a musician friend to help you. (The notes you see on the staff do not show exact musical pitches but rather indicate high, low, or medium tones played on each drum. The metronome markings offer approximate speeds, as these can vary.) The resources in the back of the book will also lead you to further explorations of these musical traditions.

If you find yourself tapping along as you read, that's good. That's what drum stories are all about. You too can learn this magical, mysterious, and powerful language that speaks to us as it has to all people since the very beginning of human civilization.

INUIT

Inuit is the name that some of the native people of the Northwest Territories of Canada, where this tale originates, call themselves. Sometimes the name is also used to designate people in all Far North groups. The word simply means "the people." The Canadian Inuit are closely related to other Native American groups of the Far North such as the Inupiat and the Yupik of Alaska and the Yüit of Siberia and St. Lawrence Island. Anthropologists believe that the Inuit have lived in the Arctic since at least four thousand years ago, when large groups migrated over a land bridge from Siberia, Mongolia, and northeastern Asia.

Over the centuries, the Inuit people developed a way of life that is suited to the cold and icy conditions of the Arctic. Traditionally, they survived mainly on hunting seal, whale, and caribou. The women stayed close to the igloos (snow houses), taking care of the children, making clothes, and preparing food from the game brought in by the men, who did most of the hunting and fishing. Despite the harsh conditions they lived in, the Inuit people developed rich traditions of art, storytelling, and music that are still important to them today.

Playing the drum is a central part of Inuit life, whether in a community-wide hunting ceremony, an individual curing ritual, or for sheer entertainment. Drums accompany the songs, chants, and games that carry Inuit traditions into the present day. There is a saying: "To stop the Inuit from singing and dancing is like cutting the tongue out of a bird."

The word for "drum" in the Inuit language is *qilaut* (*quay*-lout). Most Inuit drums are in the family called frame drums. The skin of the typical Inuit drum, which is often made of the inner membrane of a whale or walrus, is stretched over a ring of driftwood that looks like a hoop and lapped around with a taut cord of braided sinew. The drums sometimes have ivory handles and are played with sticks. In traditional Canadian Inuit society, it was the shaman, or *angakok* (an-gah-kok), who was most adept in drumming. He played the rhythms to cure the sick, to predict the whereabouts of whale and other game, or even to help his spirit travel to distant places. There are many Inuit myths about the power of song and music to help people overcome adversity, gain courage, or invoke guardian spirits' aid in hunting or in times of danger.

In the Inuit drumming style, usually one drumming phrase will accompany a song, following the line of the melody. Here is an example of an Inuit drum rhythm that was played during a "drum fight." Each player would sing, ridiculing the other players, accompanying himself on a circular frame drum with this rhythm:

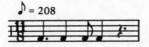

Today, many Inuit traditions have been influenced by modern technology and contact with European and Anglo-American culture over the past four centuries. But the songs and traditions are still taught to young Inuit children and used as part of their community life. Whether the drum is made of nylon stretched over a ready-made hoop or of walrus skin over driftwood, its rhythms are still woven into the life, culture, and stories of native Arctic peoples today.

frame drum

Skeleton Woman

🔰 🔰 🔰 There was an Inuit couple who had only one daughter. When she was grown, her mother and father told her it was time to marry. But the girl refused.

"I do not wish to marry anyone," she said. "I want to stay here with you. This is my home." Her parents begged and pleaded, but she wouldn't listen to them. Day after day she sat stubbornly by the fire with her arms crossed in front of her, refusing their pleas.

Many young men came to court her. All the great hunters, the best and the bravest, appeared at the igloo, carrying soft sealskins, caribou hides, and robes of ptarmigan feathers as gifts, but she would have none of them. She sat by the fire with her arms crossed and would not even speak with them.

Then one day, as the last rays of the Arctic sun began to fade from the sky, two young hunters appeared at the door. They were dressed all in white. The young girl stared at the two brothers. She had never seen such young men before. They seemed mysterious to her in their silence, and she was drawn to them. The young girl said to her parents, "I will leave you now. I am going with these two hunters."

The young woman went out into the night with the two brothers. She followed them as they stalked out of the village and onto the ice. Faster and faster they walked; faster and faster she ran to catch up with them. And suddenly, before her eyes, the two young men began to change. Their white robes slipped off. Their shoulders hunched over. She reached out to touch their hands and felt sharp claws and heavy paws instead of fingers and skin. The two brothers had become what they really were, what they had always been—polar bears of the ice world.

The girl screamed as they dragged her faster and faster over the ice. Her hood ripped and flew into the wind. Her long hair streamed behind her. "Let me go!" she cried. And they did let her go. Down and down they pushed the young woman through a hole in the ice. And down and down she fell, sinking into the cold waters of the ocean. When she reached the ocean floor, all the sea creatures began to swim around her. At first they seemed friendly, nuzzling her as they circled around. Then one fish bit her arm. Another bit her leg. Little by little the fish bit at her flesh until she was only bones. There was nothing left of her but a skeleton.

Skeleton Woman began to swim. It was dark at the bottom of the ocean. But far above, she saw a dim light shining through the waters.

"I will go that way," she said to herself. Skeleton Woman swam through the icy waters toward the light until finally she emerged through the hole. Skeleton Woman looked around. She was on land again.

There was nothing around her. For miles and miles on toward the horizon, all she could see was ice and snow. There was no village. There were no people. She was alone.

As she sat on the ice, Skeleton Woman began to remember. She remembered her parents' home and the platform outside where they kept the caribou meat to dry. She remembered her father's spear, which he used for hunting seal and fish. Skeleton Woman fell asleep and dreamed of all these things.

In the morning, when she woke up, there before her was an igloo, like the one she had grown up in. There was the platform holding caribou hides. And there was the spear, just like the one her father used for hunting seal and fish. Skeleton Woman picked up the spear. All that day she hunted near the hole in the ice. In the evening she fed herself and fell asleep. She dreamed of the twine and ivory needles her mother used for sewing hides. She dreamed of the stone lamps, and the whale oil they used to light them. She dreamed all these things, and in the morning everything was there. And slowly, slowly, Skeleton Woman built her home on the ice, just as she remembered her parents' house to be.

But she was lonely, for no people ever came.

One day, some hunters were traveling far from their village, looking for caribou. They traveled a long way over the ice, tracking through the snow and wind. Skeleton Woman could see them in the distance as they approached. At first they looked like two black dots, but as they came closer she could see they were hunters.

She ran and called to them. "See me! I am here!" she cried. At first the hunters came to greet her, but when they saw she was a skeleton, they ran away.

"No one will ever come to me here," she thought sadly, "for they will always see I am nothing but a skeleton woman. I will always, always be alone."

When the hunters returned home, they saw their father. He was an old man now, very old. It was time for him to leave his family, to end his life by going out on the ice. But his sons took pity on him. "Father," they said, "if you go out walking toward the North Star, you will see a skeleton woman there. Perhaps she will take you in."

The old man started out. Once again, Skeleton Woman saw a black dot moving on the horizon.

And once again it took shape as it came closer. Once again, she looked to see who it was. Just as night fell, the old man reached the door of her igloo. Skeleton Woman beckoned him in.

Inside, the stone lamps were lit. There was some dried fish on the floor. While the old man ate, he stared at Skeleton Woman. She looked at the old man. Then she said, "Make me a drum."

She handed him a round wooden hoop and softened walrus skin. The old man took the hoop and began to thread a hole in the skin. Patiently, patiently, with the ivory needles, he wound the walrus skin around the hoop. When the skin was tight enough, he gave the drum back to Skeleton Woman. Silently she dimmed the light from the stone lamps. And in the dark of night, Skeleton Woman began to play the drum.

As she played, she danced, circling the floor. As she played, she sang the women's song, the song she remembered her mother singing.

"Aay ya, aay ya, aay ya." She danced and danced, swaying to the rhythm of the drum as she played and played. When she was done, she turned up the light of the stone lamps. And there before her was no old man, but a powerful hunter with long black hair and flashing eyes, dressed in sealskin—young and strong.

And again Skeleton Woman dimmed the stone lamps. She played the drum. She played the drum and danced to the beat of the song her mother had taught her so long ago: "Aay ya, aay ya, aay ya." All through the night she danced and sang, beating time with her feet—circling slowly around as the drum sounded stronger and stronger. Finally, Skeleton Woman stopped drumming. She stopped dancing. When she relit the lamp, she was whole again, restored to full human form. Now dressed in a soft white robe woven from ptarmigan feathers, her long black hair streamed down her shoulders. The drumming and the dance had restored her body and made the old man young again.

In the dawn light, they walked together over the ice till they reached the village. The hunters and their families saw them coming. But they did not recognize the old man or the woman who was with him.

"I am your father," he said to them. "I was old and about to die. This woman was a skeleton. But now we are whole and young again. She will be my wife." And they walked off together, carrying the drum between them, to find another home.

HAITI

The country of Haiti is the western half of the Caribbean island of Hispaniola, a name given to it by Columbus when he arrived there in 1492. The history of this island is long and complex. First inhabited by the Arawak peoples, it was later colonized by the Spanish, and then by the French. In 1697, the island was divided. The French-speaking part (first called Saint Domingue) became Haiti; the Spanish-speaking part to the east became what is now the Dominican Republic. After a successful slave rebellion launched in 1791, the country finally became independent of the French in 1804, making it the second-oldest republic of the New World.

In Haiti, as in other parts of the Caribbean, African traditions brought by slaves from all over the west coast and central part of Africa mixed and mingled with Arawak and European influences. Together they created new languages, new religions, and new forms and styles of music. In the music called *kongo*, for example, several drums are played together while singers chant in Creole. Creole is itself a mixture of African languages, French, and trade languages. Dancers dance in honor of the *loa* (*loh*-ah), the spirits of the Haitian belief system called *vodou* (voh-doo). The drummers play, usually using a combination of three drums and an iron bell, called the *ogan* (oh-*gahn*). The largest of these drums is called the *manman* (mah-*mah*); the middle one, *segon* (seh-*gone*); and the small drum, the *boula* (*boo*-lah), that is played with sticks. Drums in Haiti have many different names, but these are the ones most commonly used for kongo music. All the drums are single headed and barrel shaped, somewhat similar to the conga drum used in Latin and rock bands. They are made of wood, often carved with intricate designs. Drum-making in Haiti is a high art; many complicated steps, procedures, and rituals are associated with it. The rhythmic pattern of kongo, in standard notation, looks like this:

*~ = *glissande* or *siyé*

Haitian rhythms share similarities with many other types of rhythms played throughout the Caribbean and Latin America. When, as in the kongo music above, several different drum patterns are played at the same time, it is called *polyrhythm*. Much of the music that had it roots in West Africa and was spread throughout the New World by people of African descent is polyrhythmic.

In the United States, slave owners often prohibited their slaves from having drums, so these styles were transferred in African–American music into complex clapping and singing patterns that in some areas, such as the Georgia Sea Islands, came to be known as "pattin' Juba." These forms of musical expression became the foundations of blues, gospel, jazz, and the rap music of today. There is also historical evidence that some African drumming traditions in North America did survive intact. The modern drum set has its origins in these earlier musical forms.

Haitian drummers use all kinds of techniques to create different tones on their drums. Often a drummer will hit the head of the drum with his hands, but sticks are used as well. When the drummer slides his thumb and index finger across the skin of the drum, a whistling sound called a *siyé* (see-*ay*), or *glissande*, is created. It is amazing to hear the varieties of sound that even a single drummer can create when all these possible combinations are played together.

In addition to religious uses, drums are a part of

Haitian folk and popular music, accompanying bands that play at parties, weddings, concerts, and festivals. Haitian children learn to play by watching and imitating the adult drummers. Sometimes they will be invited to play a stick part or a bell pattern. When they have mastered enough of these basic rhythms, some children will go on to learn until, as adults, they too can take their place in a full drumming ensemble.

asotó

The Elephant King's Drum

Adapted from Harold Courlander's tale
"Merisier, Stronger Than the Elephants"

🔔 🔔 🔔 *Krik! Krak!* In the mountainsides of northern Haiti, a farmer lived with his wife and three sons—Jean-Claude, Aristide, and Brizé. All his life he worked hard, growing coffee, plantains, and bananas in his fields and selling them in the marketplace of the nearby town of Fort-Liberté. One day, while working in his garden, the farmer fell deathly ill. As he lay on the hard wooden bed in their house, he called his sons to him and said, "My children, soon I am going to die. Soon my spirit will be with your ancestors. Now tell me, my oldest son, Jean-Claude, how will you bury me?"

And Jean-Claude said, "Father, I will bury you in a coffin made of finest mahogany, cut from the strongest tree."

"Ah, that is good," said the old farmer. Then he turned to his second son. "Aristide, my son, now that I am near death, how will you bury me?"

And Aristide said, "Father, I wish you to live long, but if you are really to die, I will bury you in a coffin made of shining brass."

Then the farmer turned to Brizé and said to him, "And you, my youngest, since I am soon to die, how would you bury me?"

And Brizé said, "Father, if you are really to die, I would bury you in the king of the elephants' drum."

"That is a fitting coffin for me!" the old farmer said. "And that is how I wish to be buried. Go, Brizé, my youngest son, and do not rest until you bring home the king of the elephants' drum."

Brizé left his father and walked sadly off to say

good-bye to his wife and small children. "It would have been better if I had offered to bring him a coffin of gold or silver!" he said to himself. "How can I ever find the king of the elephants' drum? There is an old story about it that I heard as a child, but where to find that drum, or the elephants, I do not know!"

Nevertheless, Brizé had made a solemn promise to his father, so he set off on his journey, carrying a sack with corn bread, plaintains, and mango, which his wife had prepared for him. As he walked along, he asked people in the towns and markets, "Do you know where I can find the king of the elephants' drum?" But no one had an answer for him. In the evening, as night was falling, Brizé saw a blind beggar sitting by the edge of the road. "Do you have any food for me?" the sightless man asked him. Without hesitation, Brizé reached into his sack and gave the beggar a piece of corn bread.

"If only you could see," he said sadly, "perhaps you could tell me where to find the king of the elephants' drum!" But the beggar said nothing, so Brizé went on until he found a place to rest.

The next day, again, he set off down the road, asking any passersby if they knew where to find the king of the elephants, but the men, the women, the children all shook their heads. Toward nightfall, Brizé saw a beggar with one foot resting by the roadside. "Can you share some food with me?" the crippled man asked, and without waiting an instant,

Brizé reached into his sack and gave him another piece of the bread his wife had prepared for him.

"You have only one foot, while I have two. Yet what good are my feet to me if I cannot fulfill my dying father's wish and bring him the elephant king's drum?" Then he continued on his way and found a place to rest for the night.

The next day he set out again, trudging through the twisted mountainside paths. This time he met no one on his way, until at nightfall he saw an old man sitting on a large rock by the roadside. The old man looked tired and hungry. Without even waiting to be asked, Brizé reached into his sack and handed him his last piece of corn bread. "Thank you," said the old man. "Thank you for this third piece of bread."

"Oh, no, you are mistaken," Brizé replied. "I have given you only one piece of bread."

"Not so," said the old man, "for I was the blind beggar, and I was the lame man, too. I know what you are looking for and why you are traveling so far from home. For your kindness, I will help you find the king of the elephants' drum!"

Brizé watched as the old man took out a rattle covered with beads—the sacred *ason* (ah-*sun*). He closed his eyes, and began to chant, shaking it in all four directions. Now Brizé understood that this was no ordinary old man. This was an *oungan* (oohn-*gahn*), a priest of vodou with many magical powers.

As he sang and chanted, the priest's spirit flew out of his body, ranging far across the land and then back again. When the old man put down his rattle, he opened his eyes and said to Brizé, "You must travel across the grasslands, far to the south, until you see a clearing. Many trees have been cut down there, but one remains—it is the sacred tree, the great mapou tree. They call it Mapou Plus Grand Passé Tout, the Largest Mapou of All. The elephants will come there, with their king, to drum and to dance. They will carry with them their own *asotó* (ah-so-*toh*), the giant footed drum that is as tall as a man. Watch and wait: After the elephants fall asleep, you must take the drum and run. Do not look back, but if you feel danger, take one of these *wari* nuts that I give you." The old man placed four round nuts into Brizé's palm. "Throw one of them over your shoulder and call out my name. Say, 'Merisier is stronger than the elephants!' And you will be protected."

Brizé thanked the priest many times and rushed down the mountainsides, and over the grasslands toward the south, until he found himself in a large clearing. All the trees had been cut down. The land was deserted, except for one huge mapou tree that stood with its twisted branches reaching toward the sky. It was near midnight. Small glinting lights flashed around the tree and then disappeared. Brizé was afraid, but he hid nearby, and soon, as the moon rose higher in the sky, he heard the sound of a hundred thundering feet and the blast of trumpeting calls. It was the king of the elephants and his herd, coming to dance by the mapou tree.

Brizé watched in awe as the king of the elephants himself played the great *asotó* drum, while the elephants danced and swayed, and the moon rose in the sky. Toward dawn, the elephants fell asleep by the roots of the tree. Brizé carefully, quietly, picked his way among them until he reached the king of the elephants himself, who also lay in slumber. Softly, ever so softly, he lifted up the great drum, balanced it on his head, and began to walk, then run, out of the clearing, north, through the grasslands, toward home.

At daybreak the elephants awoke. They saw their drum was gone. "We have been robbed!" cried the elephants. And immediately the herd went after the thief.

Brizé did not turn around. He did not look back. He reached into his pocket, found one of the wari nuts, and threw it over his shoulder, crying, "Merisier is stronger than the elephants!"

Instantly, a forest of pine trees sprang up. "Go through it! We must catch him!" cried the king. The elephants pushed their way through the forest with their sharp tusks and charged ahead in fury.

Brizé heard them coming closer. Once again he reached into his pocket and threw a wari nut over his shoulder, crying, "Merisier is stronger than the elephants!" This time, a raging river appeared behind him.

"Swim across!" cried the elephant king. "He has stolen our drum!" The elephants swam through the rushing waters, lifting their trunks high, until, shivering and stamping, they reached the other side.

Meanwhile, Brizé ran on, with the drum heavy on his shoulders, until he saw the mountains of the north ahead of him. Nearing home, he ran faster when again he heard the thundering sound of the elephants giving chase. "Merisier is stronger than the elephants!" he cried, throwing the third wari nut behind him.

And instantly there appeared a huge saltwater lake.

"Drink it up!" ordered the king. "Drink it up so we can cross!" All the elephants gathered around the shores of the lake. They dipped their trunks into the water to drink. But the salt water was poison for them, and one by one they died. All except the king. He alone was left, mourning his herd.

Brizé ran with the *asotó*, panting with every breath, into the mountains, past Fort-Liberté, until he reached his father's home. And whom should he see standing in the fields, with his hoe in his hands, working in the hot sun as he always did—but his father!

"Ah, Brizé, my good son, you went all that way

to bring me the drum. But as you can see, I don't need it anymore. I'm well now. Maybe you should go inside the house and rest."

Brizé carefully took the drum off his head and put it down near the garden. Then he went inside his father's house to sleep. In his sleep he dreamed of the old man, Merisier. He dreamed of the giant mapou tree. He dreamed of the great herd of elephants, sleeping under the moon and charging after him as he ran with the drum. Suddenly, he awoke with a start. He could feel the ground shaking and he heard an angry trumpeting call. It was the king of the elephants following him to the end!

Brizé reached into his pocket. He had one, only one, last wari nut. Quickly he stood up and threw it over his shoulder, calling out, "Merisier is stronger than the elephant king!" Instantly, the great drum exploded and broke into many pieces, each one becoming another, smaller drum. When he reached the edge of the fields, the elephant king himself burst apart. Each falling piece became a drummer.

Brizé watched as the drummers picked up their drums. Each drummer began to sing his own song and play his own rhythm. One by one they traveled down the mountainside and all over the country. And that is why today in Haiti you see so many drummers, each with his own drum. And that is also why it is said that to this very day, no one is buried in a drum. *Krik! Krak!*

The drum I have incorporated in this story is the *asotó* drum. It is a large, single-headed drum carved from wood and covered with cow skin. An *asotó* can be as much as six feet high. Among the Haitians, it is believed that the *asotó* has its own spirit—Outo, the spirit of the drum. It is usually played during its own sacred ceremony, but today it can be part of public dance performances as well. Frisner Augustin, a master drummer from Haiti, told me that during these ceremonies the spirit of the *asotó* is so strong it will sometimes enable dancers to leap up as high as the drum itself. The beaded *ason* rattle is also used as part of the rich and many-faceted rituals of vodou.

This story was first recorded and written down by Harold Courlander, a noted folklorist and author. Since there are no elephants in Haiti, Mr. Courlander believes that this story probably originated in West Africa and was preserved and transformed through oral transmission, gradually taking on the distinct new elements of Haitian language, culture, and values.

AKAN/GHANA

If a town becomes broken, it is the fault of the drummer.
If a town stands firm, it is due to the drummer.

—Akan proverb

The country of Ghana, on the west coast of Africa, is made up of people of widely diverse cultures and ethnic groups. The word *Ghana* itself comes from a great empire of that same name, which flourished north of present-day Ghana from the sixth to the eleventh centuries. In Ghana today, due to the years of colonial occupation by the British, English is the commonly shared language, but it is not the only one used. More than forty languages are spoken by peoples such as the Ga, the Dagomba, the Mamprusi, and the Ewe. By far the largest culture and language group of Ghana consists of Akan-speaking peoples such as the Fanti, the Akwapim, and the Ashanti, who occupy the central and southern areas of the country.

In all parts of Ghana (and indeed throughout the entire continent of Africa), drumming, singing, and dance have been integral aspects of culture for centuries, and continue to be so today. Drummers in Akan society are accorded the highest respect. It is the master drummer who has been instructed in the history, legends, proverbs, poetry, and protocol that inform every aspect of traditional life.

The master drummer knows what rhythms to play when the chief arrives to greet his community. His rhythms instruct the dancers when to change their steps or move to another beat. The master drummer addresses the spirits, and it is through him, at times, that the spirits themselves will speak. He is the custodian of the people's ancient wisdom and knowledge. Drumming is at the very heart of the Akan way of life, and music is a form of expression that is shared by young and old alike, no matter what their level of skill or ability.

Children learn drumming in Ghana by being part of the community's life, daily work, and celebrations—all of which have their own forms of musical accompaniment. Often, even very young children will create their own bands, using homemade instruments of bamboo, cans, and sticks. The rhythms they play will reflect the many styles they hear around them, like these patterns of *kpanlogo* (*pahn-lo-go*), a traditional recreational music of the Ga people of central-southern coastal Ghana.

Even young children seven, eight, and nine years of age are sometimes allowed to learn and practice the *atumpan* (ah-toom-*pahn*)—the "talking drums"— that are used by the master drummer at important ceremonies. In Ghana, drums are used not only to create musical sounds but also to "speak," imitating the tones and syllabic patterns of the local languages. So, for example, an Akan drummer might begin a ceremony honoring the chief with a poem inviting the blessings of the spirit of the drum.

Tweneboa kodua,	Wood of the drum,
Kodua tweneduro,	Wood of the drum,
Tweneduro, wo do baa bi,	Wood, if you have been away,
Merefrew yese bra.	I am calling you; we say come.
Meresua ma menhu.	I am learning, let me succeed.
Meresua ma menhu.	I am learning, let me succeed.

By using two *atumpan*—one pitched high, the other pitched low—the drummer can be understood by most listeners exactly as if he were talking to them. The first two lines would be played like this:

L = low drum
H = high drum

L   L   HL   H   LH
Twe - ne - boa   ko - dua

H   LH   L   L   H   H
Ko - dua - twe - ne   du- ro

Drum poetry is considered to be one of the highest forms of language and communication. It is played to accompany the appearance of the chief, who is at the highest level of the Akan social hierarchy. At other times, students are taught mnemonic syllables (syllables that have no real meaning, but correspond only to different drum strokes and sounds) in order to remember and play various instrumental patterns. For example, in the Ewe music called *Gahu* (gah-*hoo*) the *axatse* (ah-*hah*-tsay) or gourd rattle part is learned by repeating syllabic phrases, like this:

In the up stroke, the rattle hits the palm of the hand.
In the down stroke, the rattle hits the knee.

The *kidi* (*kee*-dee), a medium-pitched drum played with sticks, goes:

When the drum part is played together with the bell part, it is said that the two instruments are having a "conversation," which looks like this:

Throughout the country, drums are played at times of joy and sorrow, speaking the languages of dance, song, poetry, and ritual that continue to tell the stories of all Ghana's peoples.

donno

Anansi and the Secret Name

Adapted from Harold Courlander's tale "Sky God's Daughter"

🪕 🪕 🪕 We do not mean, we do not really mean, that everything you're about to hear is the truth. A story, a story! Let it come, let it go!

Long ago among the Ashanti, there lived a chief named Otuakenten. Among his children he had many sons, but only one daughter, and he guarded her jealously. When she came of age, one man after another asked to wed her, but he refused them all. The people said to one another, "This is not right. It is not fitting. Why is the chief preventing his only daughter's marriage?"

One year, during a harvest festival, the chief appeared before his people. As he made his way through the crowd, the *fontomfrom* (*fon*-tum-from) drums played loudly, announcing his arrival. As he

sat on his black stool, the master drummer stood by
the *atumpan* and began to address the crowd with a
poem:

> The path has crossed the river.
> The river has crossed the path.
> Which is the elder?
> We made the path and found the river.
> The river is from long ago,
> From the Creator of the Universe.

An elder approached the spokesman of the chief
and said to him: "Honored Otuakenten. Today we
are celebrating the harvest, but the people are puzzled and confused. You have an only daughter. One
of our sons must be worthy enough to wed her.
Why do you keep her hidden when it is time to be
considering her marriage?"

The chief replied, and the spokesman repeated
his words: "My daughter is like the sun in the morning. I have many sons, but she alone is closest to my
heart. I will give her in marriage only to one who is
very wise and very knowledgeable. I will give her in
marriage only to someone who is astute and fearless.
All these years I have kept her hidden away. Now I
say to you, I will give her in marriage only to the
one who can discover her name. These are my
words."

The news went buzzing through the crowd. The

next day in the marketplace, everyone gathered to speak of it. Who among them would guess her name? Many suitors came before the chief.

"Is her name Akosuwa?"

"Is her name Ekua?"

"Is her name Amadoma?"

But none could guess, and they were all sent away in disgrace.

Now, sooner or later, as it always does, the news about the chief's daughter came to the ears of Kwaku Anansi, the spider. Anansi said to himself, "I am the cleverest. I've always been the cleverest. Of course I will discover her name and announce it in front of the chief and all the people!"

Anansi thought for a while. Then he hit upon a plan. He knew that every day the chief's daughter went walking with her servants in the garden behind the royal palace. That morning, before the sun rose, he found his way to the garden and hid himself high in a mango tree. In a little while, the chief's daughter came walking with her servants behind her. As they approached the tree, Anansi shook one of the branches and a mango fell to the ground.

"Oh, look, Beduasemanpensa!" said the servant. "Here is a mango for you." And she handed the fruit to the chief's daughter.

They turned to go, but once again Anansi shook a branch, and another mango fell to the ground.

"Oh, look, Beduasemanpensa! Here is another mango for you!" And she picked it up.

Again they turned to go, but Anansi needed to hear her name one more time, so he shook another branch, and when the mango fell, he heard the servant say again, "Look, Beduasemanpensa, another mango has fallen! We will have sweet fruit to eat today!" And the two walked off together.

Now Anansi had heard her name three times, but he wanted to make sure he wouldn't forget it. Over and over he repeated the name to himself. "Beduasemanpensa! Beduasemanpensa!" He muttered it over and over, and when he reached his home he poured a libation of palm wine, and prayed to his ancestors to help him remember the name.

As he repeated her name to himself, Anansi began to think about how he would reveal himself as the one who had discovered it. He wanted to announce himself in a way that the chief and all the people would hear loudly and clearly—in a way that could not be mistaken. He also wanted to make sure that everyone knew for miles around how wise and clever he was to have guessed it, and so he decided to play her name on a talking drum.

But which drum to use? He looked around his house and saw his two *atumpan*. But they were so heavy. Anansi didn't want to have to carry them all the way to the palace. He saw the *apentemma* (ah-*pen*-teh-mah), but that did not have the right sound to play such an important message for the chief. Finally his eyes lit on his *donno* (*duh*-noh)—the one he could hold under his arm and play while he danced and sang. "That is the drum I will carry to the chief's palace," he said to himself. So he slung the drum over his shoulder and began to practice, over and over again, the name of the chief's daughter.

Be-dua-se-man-pen-sa!
Be-dua-se-man-pen-sa!

Anansi was beside himself. No one was as clever as he! But keeping this secret all to himself was too much for him. He had to tell someone. So as he walked to the palace, he stopped by the house of his best friend, Abosom-kitsu, the lizard. Lizard was bright green in those days. Anansi saw him from far away. He couldn't wait to tell him the news.

"I alone have guessed the name of the chief's daughter!" he whispered to his friend. "See, I'm going today to play it before the chief and all the people. Her name is Beduasemanpensa! I want you to come with me as my messenger. When we get near the palace, you must go and announce to the chief that I, Kwaku Anansi, have come to reveal his only daughter's name!"

Lizard was honored with this important mission. He went with Anansi, and when they neared the palace, he ran ahead and called out, "Anansi will say the name of Otuakenten's daughter! Come to the courtyard to hear her name!"

When he heard the news, the chief came outside. He sat on his stool. The elders and all the other people came too. Anansi stood before the chief and his spokesman and said, "You have said you will give your daughter only to the most astute, wise, and fearless suitor. And that is I, Kwaku Anansi. I alone have discovered the secret! Hear the name of your daughter, O chief!"

And with that, Anansi began to play her name on the *donno*, just as he had practiced for days and days. He played,

L L H L H L   L L H L H L
Be - dua - se - man - pen - sa————Be - dua - se - man - pen - sa

The chief looked puzzled.

"What are you saying?" he said through his spokesman. "What are you talking about?"

But Anansi just continued to play on his *donno*—"Be dua se man pen sa, Be dua se man pen sa."

The chief shook his head. "What are you talking about? I can't understand a word of that noise you are making!"

And the people turned to each other. "What is Anansi doing? What is he talking about?"

Anansi said, "I am playing her name on my *donno*! I have told it to the lizard!"

Anansi turned to Abosom-kitsu and said, "These people don't understand my playing! Tell them the name!"

And the lizard stepped forward and said, "O Chief Otuakenten. Anansi has instructed me to tell you that he has discovered your daughter's name. He is playing it for you now on the *donno*. Her name is Beduasemanpensa."

"Just so!" cried the chief. "That is her name, and you, lizard, have spoken it wisely and well. I have said that I will give her to the one who can say it, and that is what you have done. Who could ever understand such bad drumming? You, lizard, will be my son-in-law. You will wed my daughter!"

The people nodded. "It is true, it was lizard who said her name!"

Anansi was furious. He threw down his *donno* and began to chase lizard though the crowd. "Thief! Traitor!" he cried. He almost caught up with lizard, too, but at that moment Nyame, the sky god, took pity on Abosom and touched him so that he changed color from bright green to the brown of the earth, and then again to the red and yellow of the cloth that people wore as he ran by them in the marketplace. He disappeared into the forest, and Anansi never did find him. But that is why, to this day, Abosom-kitsu, the chameleon, changes his color. He is afraid of Anansi, who is still angry at him for speaking the name he worked so

hard to learn: the name of the chief's daughter—
Beduasemanpensa!

This has been my story. If it be bitter, or if it be
sweet, take some home with you, and let the rest
come back to me!

Although the *atumpan* are the most well-known talking drums
associated with chiefly ceremonies, many other drums can
"talk" as well. In this story I have chosen the *donno* for Anansi
to play. The hourglass-shaped *donno* is one of the most popular drums, not only in Ghana, but in Nigeria (where it is
called the *dundun*) and other West African countries as well. It
is slung over the shoulder with a strap and played under the
arm. By squeezing it with different degrees of pressure and
striking the skin with a hook-shaped stick, a drummer can
create many different tones and rhythmic patterns. The *donno*
is one of my favorite drums because of its singing, melodious
sound. According to master drummer Abraham Adzenyah,
this story is still being told among the Ashanti, and a version
of it has even been used for the lyrics of a popular song.

Akan Day Names

Names in Akan culture carry tremendous importance.
When a child is eight days old, a naming ceremony is performed, which welcomes him or her into the community.
In addition to the given name, the child will also have a
day name, signifying to everyone on which day of the
week he or she was born. There are also names for the nu-

merical order in which the child has come into the family. For example, in the story, the chief's daughter's name begins with the word *Bedua*, which means "tenth born." According to Akan belief, there is something special about a tenth-born child. (Perhaps that is why the chief was so particular about whom she would marry.) Here is a chart with the Akan day names for boys and girls. If you know what day of the week you were born, you can find out what your Akan day name would be. According to another belief in Ghana, people who are born on Wednesday are thought to be a little tricky and mischievous. Look who has Wednesday's name and you'll see why.

Day of the Week	Male	Female
Sunday	Kwasi	Akosuwa
Monday	Kwadjo	Adjua
Tuesday	Kobena	Abena
Wednesday	Kwaku	Ekua
Thursday	Yao	Yaa
Friday	Kofi	Effia
Saturday	Kwame	Amaa

FIJI

$\mathcal{T}$ he nation of Fiji is made up of about three hundred islands (only about one third of which are inhabited), some large, some small, in an area of the South Pacific east of Australia and directly north of New Zealand. Fiji was first settled, according to evidence found in archaeological remains, about thirty-five-hundred years ago by peoples migrating from Southeast Asia and what is now Indonesia. These people, called Lapiti, had a highly developed culture, known to us by the pottery that they left behind. The British explorer James Cook sailed through the islands in 1774, and it was through the writings of his crew that Fiji first became known to Europeans.

In 1874 Fiji became part of the British Commonwealth. During the nineteenth century, many laborers from India came to work on the banana, coconut, and sugar plantations. The independent nation of Fiji is made up of a mixture of ethnic groups, including indigenous Fijians, Indians, Chinese, Europeans, and more recent arrivals from other South Pacific islands. Yet the cultural traditions that were the inheritance of the original islanders remain a strong part of Fijian life today.

In Fiji, as in other island groups throughout the South Pacific, drumming was central to the organization of village and community life. Even today, the most common type of drum found throughout the South Pacific is the slit drum. Slit drums are made from logs that have been hollowed out, and can be six to twenty feet long and up to twelve feet wide. In Papua New Guinea, the slit drum is often carved with the head of a sacred animal, such as a crocodile or pig. Drummers, often working in pairs, play rhythms that are fast and intense to accompany dancing at feasts and community rituals. Here is an example of one such rhythm as played in a kind of music called *sasa*, from Western Samoa:

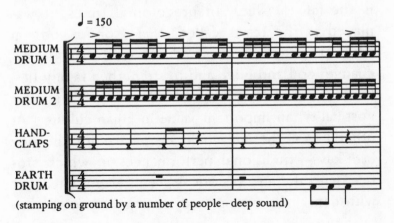

(stamping on ground by a number of people—deep sound)

In certain parts of New Guinea, it was common for each man in the village to have his own rhythm. If an urgent message had to be sent to him, a drummer would run to the village dance grounds and play that pattern. The sound of these drums could carry almost twenty miles, so wherever he might be, the person could be reached. Drums throughout the South Pacific were also used to send messages and announce important events such as births, deaths, and initiations.

In Fiji, the name of this all-important instrument is the *lali* (*lah*-lee). In precolonial times, it was played at the feasts called *solevu* (soh-*leh*-voo), at which two groups of islanders would meet to exchange food and gifts, and to strengthen family ties. (*Kani-loloma*—kah-nee-loh-*loh*-mah—is the word for hospitality, an important value in Fijian culture.) At other times, the *lali* would be played for the *meke* (*meh*-kay)—traditional performances in which stories, legends, and historical events were acted out with dance, drumming, and singing When the European missionaries came, they forbade many of these tribal traditions and ceremonies. But even today the *lali* is played on Sunday to announce church services, and every year, at Christmastime, groups of Fiji islanders travel from house to house, playing the *lali* and sharing gifts with friends and neighbors, singing and feasting sometimes straight through to the new year. Echoes of the *lali* drum can still be heard in Fiji across village squares, through forest pathways, and across the rippling waves of the Pacific.

lali

The Silent Drum of Ono Island

🝓 🝓 🝓 This story happened long ago, when, it is told, the people of Ono Island had a chief named Tui Matakono. In those days they lived from gardening, gathering coconuts and breadfruit, and fishing. The men would go out onto the blue waters of the Pacific in their boats, called *takia*, and bring back rich catches from the sea. The women worked

42 • FIJI

in the gardens or gathered the bark of mulberry trees to make *tapa*, the island cloth they decorated with beautiful designs. At night, families gathered under the thatched roofs of their houses to share meals and to drink the delicious *kava* drink, made from the island's own peppery plant.

On special occasions, the village drummer would go to the dancing ground and play the *lali* to call the people together for a solevu. After making a speech, Tui Matakono would sit and watch as his people celebrated—dancing out legends, or praising his own wisdom and exploits in battle. In the days of Tui Matakono, time passed peacefully for the people of Ono Island.

Ono Island had its own deity, whom the people called Liga Mudu—the one-armed god. At a feast or celebration he was always honored and remembered with dances, prayers, and offerings.

One day, ships from other islands began to land on the beaches of Ono Island. Raiding parties went about from village to village, burning down houses and destroying the crops. Soon even the sacred *lali*, the village drum, had been put to the ax, and the people of Ono were left desolate and afraid. Tui Matakono called them together and said, "We must not give up hope. Let us go up to the hilltops and build forts to protect ourselves. This time of war will pass, and then we will decide what to do."

The people followed their chief's advice. They

took what few belongings they had left and went up into the mountains. In rough wooden fortresses they watched as their villages continued to burn, one by one. When the last raiding party had sailed off and the horizon was clear for many days, Tui Matakono ordered his people back down the mountain, to see what they could do to rebuild their homes.

Many houses had burned, but some remained. Many crops of yams and bananas had been destroyed, but a few fields were left. Many takias had been stolen or broken, but some survived. The people had enough to start a new life again on Ono.

But one thing was missing—the most important thing of all—the *lali* drum had been hacked to splinters. Ages ago, it had been made by one of the finest drum-makers of the island, but now it was beyond repair. Tui Matakono knew that the people of his village needed a drum. He needed the drum too, to send messages across the island or to announce important days to come. And there were no more vesi trees—the hardwood from which all *lali* drums are made—on Ono Island.

"We must go to Kambara, where all the great drum-makers are now," he said. "We must go to Kambara and see if we can trade for a *lali* drum."

"And with what shall we trade?" his advisers asked. "We have little enough left as it is, and we must use what we can to rebuild our villages."

Then a wise woman spoke up. Her name was

Mina. She had five children and even more grand-children. Mina had seen much in her day. She knew the ways of the world. And Mina said, "When I saw the raiders coming, I made sure to hide my tapa cloth in a basket under the ground, thinking we might need it someday. I will go now to find it."

Then another woman spoke up. "I too hid my tapa cloth, the one with our beautiful island designs on it. I'll go find it." One by one the women of the island called out to each other. Long ago they had made a pact that in times of trouble, they would each save something of value—and nothing was of more value to them than the delicate cloth that they dyed and decorated with loving hands, using the juice of the mulberry tree.

Soon, the men repaired their takia boats and loaded them with the bundles of tapa cloth that the women had saved and gathered. Then they set out for the island of Kambara, about a day's journey, to trade what they could for a new drum. When they reached Kambara, they were greeted in the true tra-dition of kani-loloma—with hospitality and warmth. The Kambara Islanders were impressed, too, with the beauty of the Ono cloth. They were ready to trade.

The Ono party looked over the many drums they saw displayed. Some were smooth and shiny, others were carved with intricate patterns. Some were as tall as a man, others even larger. Finally, Tui

Matakono himself, who had accompanied the men on this important mission, chose the *lali* drum for Ono. It was a smooth one, just his own height. And when the drummers beat it with their wooden mallets, its tones rang out like the voice of a god, echoing far over the waters.

The Ono traders thanked the Kambara drummakers. After carefully carrying the drum down to the shore, and binding it tightly to their best takia, they set off for home. At first the sea was calm and the winds were favorable. The boats moved swiftly on the ocean currents. But halfway through the journey, the sky darkened with clouds. A terrible storm was brewing. The waves reached higher than a man's head and lashed the sides of the takia. "We are doomed! We are lost!" cried the Ono sailors as lightning flashed across the sky and a terrifying wind churned the sea.

"We must pray," cried Tui Matakono. "We must pray to our god, Liga Mudu. Only his power can save us now."

Tui Matakono and all the men sent a fervent prayer to the one-armed god. "Save us," they wept into the wind's fury. "Save us and we will offer you a feast when we return to Ono—the greatest feast the island has ever seen, in thanks for your help. We must return to our families. We must bring the drum home to our village."

Instantly, the waters of the sea became calm. The

sun broke through the clouds, and the winds became fair. On a gentle breeze they were carried
back to the shores of Ono.

As soon as they reached home, the women and
children came to greet them on the beach, laughing
and clapping. Tui Matakono was proud of the suc-
cess of their trade and their journey. He stood on
the beach and watched with a smile in his eyes as
the islanders carried the drum up the path and back
to the village. He joined them later in the center of
the village dancing grounds. There, he instructed
four of the strongest men as they placed the drum
carefully on top of two wooden runners, so its
sound would ring out clearly when the time came to
play it. Caught up in the return of the drum and the
busy activities that followed, he forgot all about his
promise to Liga Mudu. He forgot about the feast he
had promised to the one-armed god who had saved
them on the ocean waters, and so did all the members of the crew that had gone with him to Kambara.

Days passed. The villagers planted their fields
again and replaced the thatching on the roofs of
their houses. They repaired boats and made new
ones. They set about to mend their nets and spears.
Ono was back to normal. Liga Mudu waited for his
feast. He waited many days, and then his patience
ran out.

One evening, as Tui Matakono sat outside his
house, a stranger walked through the village. No

one had ever seen him before and no one knew how he got there, for no boat had been sighted on the waters. No footprints marked the sand. He was wrapped in a soft cloak, with only one arm showing at his side. The stranger walked past Tui Matakono and onto the dancing ground. He reached his one arm toward the *lali* drum and seemed to draw something out of it as he passed by—a misty gray form, like a shadow or a wisp of smoke. And then, the stranger was gone.

Tui Matakono blinked. He shook his head. *"Sombo!"* he said. "Alas, I seem to have been dreaming. But did I not say that we would offer a feast to Liga Mudu, the one-armed god who saved us at sea many days ago? Come, it is time to play the *lali* drum that we brought with us from Kambara!"

He called his best drummer to the dancing ground. "Play the drum," he said. "Tell the people it is time now for our feast of thanks!" The drummer picked up the mallets. Anxiously, Tui Matakono waited to hear its sound, the sound that had rung out so clear and strong on Kambara. The drummer struck the *lali* once, twice, three times, but no sound came out of the drum. It was silent. Another drummer came up to try it. He struck it once, twice, three times, but the drum was mute—not a sound could be heard. Finally, Tui Matakono himself picked up the mallets. "You do not know how to play anymore. Let me try!"

He struck the drum with the mallets with all his

force and strength. Many times he played it, but the drum was silent.

The voice of the *lali* drum never returned. The people prayed and waited, but their prayers were never answered. Only sometimes, on a night just before a storm, when the wind blew hard and sent whitecaps rippling over the waters, could they hear a distant, mocking thunder, like the voice of a god, echoing over the ocean. Then they knew it was the lost voice of their island's drum—the only voice of the *lali* drum they would ever hear on Ono again.

KOREA

The homeland of the Korean people is a mountainous region about the size of Minnesota that is located on a peninsula bordered to the north by China, to the east by the Sea of Japan, and to the west by the Yellow Sea. The area is now divided between two countries, the Democratic People's Republic of Korea, or North Korea, and the Republic of Korea, or South Korea. Koreans are descendants of migratory groups who emerged from the region of Siberia, Mongolia, and inner Asia thousands of years ago. Although there have been strong influences from China and other Asian nations at various times in their history, the Korean people have clung fiercely to their own heritage, language, and customs. This strong sense of being Korean is still evident wherever Koreans live today—either in their homeland or in immigrant communities abroad.

The value of family unity and shared history is

particularly important for Koreans. Each family has its own genealogical table, written on scrolls, so that children can see their names added to a long list of relatives, stretching back for generations. Respect for ancestors, in thought and in ritual, is instilled in children from a young age. In Korean tradition each person has three names: the family name (such as Kim, Pak, or Choi); a generational name, which marks how many generations the person is descended from his or her original ancestors; and a given name, chosen for a child by a parent or grandparent, which has a unique, special meaning. In this story, the eldest son's name is Kim Hyukchin. Kim is the family name. Hyuk, meaning "brilliant," is the generational name, which all the brothers share. And chin, which means "truth," is his given name. Heirlooms, such as family scrolls, woven tapestries, or even musical instruments, are carefully maintained—usually by the eldest son—so that these treasures will always remain in the family's possession.

Korean civilization developed from early nomadic tribes to organized clan states, which later evolved into kingdoms and royal dynasties. The last of these, the Yi Dynasty, held power from 1392 all the way to 1910, when Korea was colonized by the Japanese. During these centuries, different social classes evolved in Korea. *Yangban* was the word for the aristocrats and royalty. *Sangmin* was the word for the common folk—peasants and farmers. Korean music reflected these differences. Certain styles of music would be heard only at court rituals and royal banquets, while other kinds of music were played by the sangmin for their family gatherings and communal events.

Drumming rhythms were important in all levels of society. They accompanied harvest festivals and work in the fields for the peasants, as well as the epic songs and poetic ballads that were played in the royal palaces. One of the most ancient and popular of Korean drums is called the *changgo* (*chahn*-go), which means, literally, "drum played with a stick." It is a double-headed hourglass drum cut from the hardwood of a tree called the *odong namu* (in English it is known as the paulownia). The left side of the *changgo* is covered with cow skin. Depending on the music or dance form, it is played with a stick or with the hand alone. It is considered to be the female side of the drum. The right side of the drum is covered with sheep or dog skin, and is considered to be the male side of the drum. It is struck with a thin, light bamboo stick. The drum heads are tightened on each end of the drum body by crimson cords or twine laced around metal hoops, which keep the skins in place. The drum is tuned by adjusting the tension of the cords. It can be played sitting down, as in the style of the court musician. Or, when held by a shoulder strap, it can be played marching, standing, or dancing, in the style of the working farmers. So popular is the *changgo* even today that it has been called the national drum of Korea.

Korean children learn to play the *changgo* using a combination of mnemonic syllables; each stroke or combination of strokes has its own syllable. There is also a wonderful system of notation—each sound and syllable also has a visual symbol. Here is a list of these symbols:

	Korean
tdung (left hand and right hand playing together)	①
kuk (right-hand touch)	●
kiduk (right hand, double stick)	i
kung (left hand open)	○
tdok (right hand, single stick)	|
turrrr (right hand, tremolo with stick)	⋮
tuk (right hand, end of tremolo with stick)	•
rest (silent beat)	—

Here is an example of what a drumming phrase looks like in Korean notation. Next to it you can see what it looks like in standard Western notation.

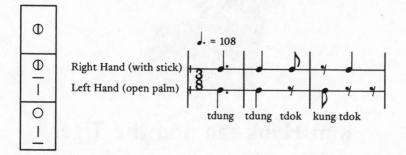

Drums can be colorfully painted in blue and red, or simply left in their natural state of polished wood. These decorations have symbolic meaning even beyond their visual beauty. The blue and red colors of the drum represent the unity of heaven and earth. Playing the two sides of the drum together signifies harmony between male and female. The lively, measured beats of the *changgo* express the ideals of harmony and balance that are so important to Korean art forms and the Korean philosophy of daily life.

changgo

Kim Hyuk-san and the Tiger

🔊 🔊 🔊 *Yennal yennal-é.* Long ago, in the early days of the Yi Dynasty, there lived in a southern province of Korea a poor farmer who had three sons, and they all carried his family name—Kim. The eldest son's name was Kim Hyuk-chin, the second son's name was Kim Hyuk-kyu, and the third son's name was Kim Hyuk-san.

Although they all worked hard on their small plot of land, life never got any better for the Kim family. By the time the old farmer was on his deathbed, they were destitute and penniless. Nevertheless, the father gathered his three sons around him and said, "My children, I have worked hard my whole life, but poverty has always been our fate. Still, I wish to leave you a legacy that will help you after I am gone. Go look in the wooden trunk in the corner, and bring me what you see inside." The three sons sadly carried the trunk to their father's bedside. He opened it and reached down.

"To you, Hyuk-chin, my eldest, I give this stone mill. It always worked well for my father and grandfather. I hope it will do the same for you." He reached inside again and pulled out an empty wine gourd and a bamboo cane. "Hyuk-kyu, my second son, the wine from this gourd always tasted sweet. May it also bring sweetness to your life." Then he reached in one more time and pulled out his own drum—the little wooden *changgo* that his father had made for him when he was a child. "Hyuk-san, I spent many happy hours singing and playing this drum. I hope it will bring you the same. Now, my sons, you each have a legacy from me. Poor though these gifts might be, do your best to use them when you go out to make your way in the world." The three children thanked their father profusely, and soon after, he died. They buried him in the family plot. And, after completing all necessary details of the funeral, they closed down their little hut and set off down the road to make their way in the world, as their father had bidden them to do.

After some time, they came to a place where the road separated in three directions. The brothers decided they would each take a different path, and at the end of a year they would meet again to see how they had managed.

Hyuk-chin took the road to the south. He traveled on past fields and forest, carrying the stone mill on his back, until at nightfall, not finding any place to sleep, he climbed up into the branches of a tree to seek shelter for the night. Toward midnight he was awakened by the sound of men shouting and yelling at one another below him. Quietly, from his hiding place in the branches, he looked down and saw a band of robbers. They were surrounded by sacks of gold they had plundered from nearby towns and villages.

"These are mine! I worked the hardest!" cried one.

"Oh, no, they're mine! This gold belongs to me!"

Quarreling as they were, they did not notice Hyuk-chin shaking in his shoes up in the tree. Suddenly, Hyuk-chin had an idea. Carefully he took the stone mill from his back and, grabbing on to the handle, began to grind it, slowly at first, then faster and faster. The sound of the grinding stones echoed through the still night air. Looking around them, the robbers were terrified. "Where is that sound coming from?" they asked one another. "How can it be thundering when there is not a drop of rain, nor a cloud to cover the moon? It must be the voices of the ancestors, who are angry with us for stealing all this gold! Let's run and leave this place while we have the chance!"

The whole lot of them ran and didn't stop till they had crossed the border into China. They were never heard from again. But as for Hyuk-chin, he descended from the tree, gathered all the sacks of gold, and made his way to the nearest town, where he set himself up as a merchant and never had to worry about his next meal again.

Hyuk-kyu took the road to the north. He had with him the wine gourd and the bamboo cane, which he used as a walking stick. When nightfall came, he found himself near a cemetery. Not being at all afraid, he found a nice soft spot next to one of the burial mounds and got ready to fall asleep. All of a sudden, he heard an eerie whistling sound, and the thud of footsteps coming closer and closer.

Hyuk-kyu hid behind the burial mound. He looked all around, but he didn't see anyone. Then, again, he heard the whistling sound, and the footsteps coming closer and closer. In the misty fog that was beginning to cover the hillside, he saw the shadow of an evil spirit coming toward him.

"Come on, Mr. Skeleton! Wake up, *baegol!* We have a job to do!" the spirit hissed. "Don't you remember? Tonight is the night we're going to steal the soul of the daughter of that wealthy scholar who lives down the road. Come on, get up—it's time to go and I need your help!" At that moment, Hyuk-kyu made up his mind what to do.

"I'm ready. Here I am," he whispered from behind the mound of earth.

"I don't recognize your voice at all," said the spirit. "Prove to me that it is you!" Gingerly, Hyuk-kyu held out the wine gourd. "Aha," said the spirit. "Round and smooth, not a hair on your head, I see! You are an old skeleton indeed. But I'm still not sure it's you. Hold out your hand!" And with that, Hyuk-kyu held out the bamboo cane for the spirit to touch. "Long and skinny, worn to the bone—it must be you then. Come along!" said the spirit, and in the misty fog, Hyuk-kyu followed closely behind the ghostly shape that floated ahead of him.

At the bottom of the cemetery, and down the road, he saw the large, spacious house of a yangban. The spirit bade him wait by the gate while it went into the darkened house. In a little while, out it came, with something cupped in its glowing hands. "Here is the girl's soul—we have her now!" Hyuk-kyu opened up the top of the wine gourd.

"Put it in here for safekeeping," he whispered. "We wouldn't want to lose it!" As soon as the spirit had taken his advice, Hyuk-kyu closed up the gourd as tightly as he could and tied it to his waist with a string. On the way back to the graveyard, he daw-dled, and kept pretending to drop things.

"Hurry up," called the spirit. "You're taking too much time!"

At that moment, a rooster crowed. Night was over; daylight began to spread across the sky. The spirit screeched and disappeared, for, as Hyuk-kyu well knew, no spirit has power after the sun has risen. He turned around and ran as fast as he could back to the house of the yangban. He saw the people there weeping and tearing their clothes in mourning.

"How could this have happened?" the family cried. "She was happy and healthy just yesterday. How could it be that she is dead?"

Hyuk-kyu approached the yangban himself and said, "I'm sorry for your distress. I have traveled in far-distant lands and have seen many cures performed for the sick and dying. Perhaps there is something I can do."

The master of the house, in desperation, led him to his daughter's room. Hyuk-kyu closed the door. Then he went to the daughter's bedside, unwound the string, opened the top of the gourd, and placed it under her nostrils. No sooner had he done so then her soul flew right back into her body, and she sat up in bed, saying, "Have I been sick? What am I doing still in bed at this hour of the morning?"

On seeing his daughter alive and well, the yangban bowed low before Hyuk-kyu, so deep was his gratitude to the young man. "How can I ever repay you for saving my daughter's life?" he said. "I believe you must be her destined bridegroom. I insist that you stay with us and agree to marry her."

And so, when the appropriate day had been chosen, Hyuk-kyu, the poor farmer's son, married the yangban's daughter, and he lived as his son-in-law in wealth and ease from that day on.

But what about Hyuk-san, the youngest one? What was his fate to be? Since his two brothers had chosen the roads to the north and the south, there was nothing left for him to do but go straight ahead. Hyuk-san was by nature a happy soul. Without a penny to his name or a crumb in his pocket, he nevertheless slung the *changgo* resolutely over his shoulder and began to march along, singing a song he remembered from his childhood:

He marched along, singing this song until the road took him high up into the mountains. Far below he could see a small village, but to his right and to his left there was nothing but a thick forest of trees.

"*Param i punda, param i punda,*" he was singing, when all of a sudden he heard a deep growling noise. He sang a little louder, "*Param i punda, param i punda.*"

The deep growling noise got louder and louder. Hyuk-san played his drum louder and louder, and just as he was about to take a turn on the path, an enormous tiger with burning yellow eyes leapt up in front of him with its claws bared.

"*Param yi punda, param i punda*"—*tdung-tdung-tdok-kung-tdok.*

Hyuk-san played with trembling hands, but he did not stop. The tiger came nearer and nearer. Hyuk-san played on for all his life, and just when it seemed that the tiger was about to pounce—the great animal stood up on its hind legs and started to dance a tigerish dance to the rhythm of the drum:

TDUNG-TDUNG-TDOK-KUNG-TDOK
TDUNG-TDUNG-TDOK-KUNG-TDOK

The tiger had never been so happy in his whole life. Finally he had some good music to dance to! As long as he played the drum, Hyuk-san had a happy, dancing tiger to keep him company on the road. Down the mountain path they went, and when they reached the village, the people ran to open the gates for him. All year long they lived in fear of the tiger, who would come down the mountain to steal their livestock and carry off their children—and here he was, dancing tamely to the beat of the *changgo* played by a mere youth. Everyone threw money and food into the sack that Hyuk-san held out for them, and merrily he went along, from town to town, with his tiger dancing around him. Wherever they went, they got the same response— applause, cheers, and plenty of food and money. After a while, the tiger calmed down and became tame even when Hyuk-san wasn't playing the drum, which was a good thing, for Hyuk-san's hands were getting tired.

After several months of these travels, word of the boy and his dancing tiger reached the ears of the king himself. The king demanded a royal court performance by the amazing pair. And so, the very next day, Hyuk-san marched into the palace, followed by his striped friend. The king was astounded. He had never heard such good *changgo* playing, and he had never seen a dancing tiger before!

"Teach me that rhythm," he commanded, "and give me that drum! I want to make the tiger dance!"

Hyuk-san refused. "This little drum is my only inheritance from my father. Out of respect for him and my ancestors, I must keep it—for see what luck it has brought me."

But the king was adamant. He had to have that drum! He begged and pleaded, but Hyuk-san still refused. Finally, the king offered him a sack of *ryang*—bronze coins. Hyuk-san shook his head. "Up to half my treasure!" the king cried. "It is yours!" Hyuk-san realized that a king is still a king, and as fine a musician as he was, he was still nothing but a humble sangmin—a peasant. He loved the tiger, and the drum, but it was hard to turn down the offer of half the king's treasure. And so, in the end, he taught the king how to play, gave the tiger a hug, thanking him for all their good times, and handed over his beloved *changgo*.

A short time later, Hyuk-san met with his brothers, as they had promised, by the roadside. They congratulated each other on all the good fortune that had befallen them since they last parted, and praised their father for the valuable legacies he had left them. In time they built their homes near to each other and continued to live in family harmony, good health, and prosperity till the end of their days.

INDIA

The huge Asian subcontinent of which India is a part is home to some of the most ancient and influential of all human civilizations. Scholars and archaeologists are still unearthing ruins of great cities that existed at least forty-five-hundred years ago in the Indus Valley. Around 1500 B.C.E., bands of migratory warriors who called themselves Aryans made a place for themselves in the northern plains. The older Dravidian culture (whose descendants make up the main ethnic groups of southern India) was absorbed into the new one. That mixture and other influences formed the basis of Hindu religion and philosophy, which still serves as a guiding force in the lives of millions of Indian citizens. In the sixteenth century, Moghul emperors and preachers brought Islam to the region. The long years of British rule also left a lasting impression on today's India.

Music and the arts have always had an important

role in Indian culture and traditions. In Hindu tradition music is considered to be one of the highest forms of spiritual expression. Instruments are featured in sculptures of the gods and goddesses adorning the walls of ancient temples. The origin of the universe itself is associated with sound and music. Drums are especially revered, and a special lore of stories and beliefs surrounds them.

In one Hindu legend, the god Shiva appeared to a great scholar, Panini (who actually lived, probably in the second century B.C.E.). Panini was trying to comprehend the secrets of Sanskrit—the holy language of Hindu scriptures. Shiva played the *dhamaru* (dah-*mah*-roo) drum for him, revealing in its rhythms all the possible combinations of the sounds in the Sanskrit alphabet. Shiva told him that understanding these rhythms would lead to the deeper knowledge of the languages, arts, and sciences that he sought, and ultimately would reveal the nature of the universe itself. The story of Panini is still told and written about in India today.

There are many kinds of drums in India. Perhaps the most well known to Americans is the *tabla* (*tahb*-la), which is played mostly in northern India. The tabla consists of two upright, single-headed drums played next to each other. South Indians often use the *mrdangam* (mur-*dahng*-ahm), a barrel-shaped two-headed drum, which is played in their Karnatic (classical) music. The *ghatam* (*gah*-tahm), a drum made from a clay pot, requires the same skill to play as the *tabla* and *mrdangam*. The small hourglass-shaped *dhamaru*—known as the monkey drum—is considered to be one of the most powerful drums of all. According to Hindu mythology, it is through this drum that the universe was created, and through it the universe will be destroyed and renewed again in the endless cycles of time.

These drum stories are part of the folklore that children in India grow up with, at home and in school. When Hindu children first go to study the drum, whether it is the *tabla* or the *mrdangam*, they will make a *puja* (*poo*-jah), an offering to Ganesh—the elephant-headed god, son of Shiva and the goddess Parvati, who is also associated with drumming and dancing—and ask for his blessings. Not only gods and goddesses, but drummers too are assumed to have unique abilities and powers. Paul Leake, an American *tabla* player, told me that in India there is a custom that if a child stutters, his parents will take him to a master drummer's house. There he will eat the rice paste that is used to cover the center of the drum's skin. Some believe that if the family goes to a truly great drummer, the cure will be successful.

Indian rhythms are extremely complex. Instruments such as the *tabla* and *mrdangam* require years of devoted study with a master teacher before a student will have enough skill to play in public. The study begins with learning the syllables, the language of the

drum. As in other traditions, each syllable corresponds to a particular drum stroke. In classical Indian music, drums are played with hands only, although stick drumming can be found in many regions of India for religious festivals and other community events. The student must learn to recite the various combinations of syllables before the correct sequence of hand strokes can be played on the drum. Although pronunciations and techniques differ slightly for the *mrdangam* and the *tabla*, common to both is the concept of *tala* (*tah*-la). Tala refers to the repeating cycle of beats—such as five, seven, or eleven—that provides the rhythmic structure for a given piece of music. Using a combination of claps, finger counts, and hand waves, listeners can keep the time cycle while the musicians play. The rhythmic patterns can be simple or complicated, but the beats of the tala remain constant. Here is an example of a South Indian *solkuttu*—a spoken rhythmic phrase set in the eight-beat cycle called *adi* (*ah*-dee) *tala*:

After learning how to clap the tala and say these rhythms many times over, it is much easier to play the patterns on the drum, despite the different fingerings and hand positions. My South Indian drumming teacher, Ramnad Raghavan, would make his students say these phrases over and over again. He would walk around and tap us on the head if we weren't concentrating, saying, "Keep the tala!" And soon enough, we were ready to play.

tablas

Shiva and the Ash-Demon

Din din na ... din kirikita din na
Din din na ... din kirikita din na

In the beginning of the world, the god Shiva ruled on high from his home on Mount Khailash. A shaman, warrior, and mystic, Shiva would sit in deep meditation. Covered in sacred white ashes, with his companion snakes draped around his shoulders and his trident beside him, he would gaze with his third eye, the eye of wisdom, deep into the secrets of the universe. With the flaming fire of this eye, he could destroy the world with a glance, but Shiva understood its power, and knew how to use it wisely.

In those times, the gods and goddesses lived in peace and harmony. Anything they wished for would appear before them, for in their heavenly home they knew only bliss and well-being. In the world just below theirs lived the *asuras* (ah-*sur*-ahs), the demons. The demons too had many powers, but they were jealous and unhappy, for although they lived near the roots of the tree of knowledge and wisdom, they could never taste its fruits.

There was one demon, though, whose devotion to Shiva was boundless. His name was Bhashmashur, and he was known as the ash-demon. For thousands of years, Bhashmashur followed the ascetic practices of yoga in worship of Shiva. For a thousand years he stood on a mountaintop with his arms raised to the skies without moving. For another ten thousand years he never tasted food, and drank only sips of water from an underground spring. For aeons and aeons he traveled the world as a beggar, without ever sitting down. And at the end of all that time, after these many acts of spiritual discipline, Bhashmashur appeared before Shiva and asked him for a boon—a reward.

Shiva knew that Bhashmashur was still a demon.

But after all Bhashmashur had done in self-denial and penances, Shiva also knew that he could not refuse his request. From the height of Mount Khailash, he looked down at Bhashmashur gently and said, "Yes, Bhashmashur, for your years of devotion, fasting, and prayer, I will fulfill your wish. What do you request of me?" Bhashmashur took a deep breath, for this was the moment he had been waiting for through all the centuries and aeons of time.

"Give me the power of your third eye," he said. "I wish to have it so that I too can gaze into the secrets of the universe and command all that I see."

Shiva smiled a little to himself. Then he reached out and touched Bhashmashur on the tip of his finger. "Your wish has been fulfilled. You have your boon."

Bhashmashur leapt down to the demon world, his bloodshot eyes flashing, his fangs bared.

"Aha!" he cried. "Now I am the most powerful of asuras! For Shiva has given me the power of his third eye!" One of the asuras had displeased him recently. He pointed his finger at him and the demon instantly burst into flames and turned to ashes. The other asuras drew back in horror.

"Nothing can stop me now!" cried Bhashmashur. He flew down to the earth, the realm of humans, and pointed his finger at a mountain. Immediately it burst into flames and turned to ashes. The humans cowered in fear and awe. "I, Bhashmashur, am now ruler of the earth!" he cried. And even into the highest realm, where the gods lived in perfect bliss and contentment, Bhashmashur ranged among the gardens and the meadows, pointing his finger and turning their world to dust.

Finally, in desperation, the gods and goddesses appealed to Shiva. "You must do something about Bhashmashur!" they implored. "You have given him this boon, and now he is destroying the world with his power to send everything up in flames!"

Shiva listened to them calmly, and then he spoke. "I will take care of this. I will find a way to deal with Bhashmashur. Now leave me in peace."

The deities left, and Shiva returned to his meditations. Deep in trance, he gazed with his eye of wisdom until he saw what he was looking for. Still in trance, he flew out of his body, with the crescent moon shining from his matted locks. Covered in sacred ashes, he came to the edge of the Indian Ocean. There, floating upon the beach, was a *coco de mer*, a sea coconut—the rare fruit that washes up onto the shores of India all the way from Madagascar. Shiva picked up the sea coconut, and with the flame of his third eye he sliced it in half. He covered each half with skin from the snakes that encircled his body, and began to play. From the drum on his right there came the sound of birds singing, of brooks bubbling, of leaves rustling in the breeze. All the creatures of the world stopped to hear his music. And when he struck the drum on the left, there came the sound of the earth shaking, of booming thunder, of trees cracking in a storm. And this was the very first *tabla* drum.

Shiva picked up the drum he had made and flew back to Mount Khailash. There he sent out a message to the gods and goddesses, to the asuras, the demigods, and all the celestial beings: "When the next full moon rises, I will be giving a feast and a party. You are all to come!"

And because the invitation was from Shiva himself, all did come. When the next full moon rose in the sky, Shiva opened up his palace to his guests. Soon the gods and goddesses arrived. There was Sarasvati, goddess of knowledge and the arts, riding a white swan, and Vishnu the Preserver, floating on a bed of snakes. There came four-headed Brahma the Creator, and Indra, accompanied by his court musicians—the *gandarva*s and the *apsara*s. Shiva's beautiful consort, Parvati, the daughter of the Himalayas, was there to greet them, and Ganesh, their son, played merrily with his friends. After the gods and goddesses entered, the spirits, demons, and demigods from the other realms of the cosmos came onto the mountaintop as well—and, of course, being an asura himself, Bhashmashur was among them.

When Bhashmashur entered, the other guests drew back in fear. Threatening them with menacing glances, he curled and uncurled his long-nailed fingers as he strode past the crowd, but out of respect for Shiva he did not set anything on fire.

Shiva and Parvati motioned everyone to be seated while the most delicious food and drinks were served. The stars themselves served as torches, shining their light into the hall, and the sweet fragrance of incense filled the air.

At the end of the feast, Shiva lifted up a tiger skin and revealed the drums he had made. With his audience gathered around him, Shiva began to play. The melody of the drums was like nothing they had ever heard before. The sounds of the oceans, of rivers, of the spinning wheels of time itself rippled out from his fingers in the magical tones of the drum. Hypnotized by the beauty of its rhythms, the gods and goddesses, the demons and demigods—all who were there—listened in awe and wonder. And then Parvati, the most beautiful of all the goddesses, the beloved consort to Shiva, stood up and began to dance. As she twirled and stamped to the rhythms of the *tabla*, the guests were completely spellbound—the power of the dance and drum held them all captive. As Shiva continued playing his rhythms, Parvati stopped dancing and gazed around. Then she said, "A dancer without a partner is like the earth without the sky, the sun without the moon. Who can dance with me? Who will be my partner? Is there anyone here who can match me step for step and gesture for gesture?"

Of all the guests, only one stood up. Only one

thought himself strong enough, powerful enough, and graceful enough to match the steps of Parvati, and that was Bhashmashur.

"I can dance with you," he said, "for my dancing is beyond compare!"

"We will see," said Parvati, and she motioned him onto the jeweled floor of the palace. "You must prove to me what a good dancer you are," she said. "I must see if you can do everything exactly as I do!"

Bhashmashur took one long look around with his glittering red eyes and waved his hands toward the deities. Again they shuddered, as Bhashmashur howled with laughter. "Only one can dance with Parvati," he crowed, "and that is I, Bhashmashur!" And with that he stepped onto the dance floor.

Parvati nodded. Bhashmashur did the same, shaking his demon locks. Parvati curled her wrists and gazed to the right. Bhashmashur stuck out his hands and blinked to the right. She curled her wrists again and gazed to the left. Bhashmashur followed with clumsy motions. Parvati stamped to the rhythms of the drum:

Ta din na—ta kirikita din na!

Bhashmashur stomped on the ground:

TA DIN NA—TA KIRIKITA DIN NA!

And all the while, Shiva smiled a little smile and continued to play, while the guests sat hypnotized by the music and the dance.

Parvati spun and twirled. Bhashmashur gallumphed around the floor. She reached out as if to pluck a delicate flower. He smacked his hand down on the floor.

Then Parvati lifted her palms to the full moon. Bhashmashur too waved at the moon. She gestured with her palms circling around her. Bhashmashur circled. She knelt down to the ground, bending low, and the demon followed. Carried away by the beauty of her movements and mesmerized by the resounding melody of the drums, he mimicked everything that she did. Finally, Parvati stretched her right arm up and pointed to the crown on her head. Bhashmashur stretched out his arm and, without thinking, pointed to himself! In that instant he burst into a cloud of fiery flames and then crumbled into ashes. As the last rhythms of the *tabla* died away, the wind picked up the ashes and blew them throughout the universe. Bhashmashur would have to live through many lives in countless worlds before he could return again.

The gods and goddesses cheered and rejoiced. The celestial musicians sang and danced for joy. Even the asuras were happy to see Bhashmashur disappear, and they all thanked Shiva and Parvati for restoring peace to their world.

And the *tabla* drums, first created by Shiva on the shores of the Indian Ocean, remain, even in our times of strife and hardship, to remind us of this story. The drum on the right still sounds like birds singing and streams rushing through the mountains. And the drum on the left still sounds like the shaking of the earth and thunderstorms. Listen to a master drummer play, and you'll hear it too . . .

> *Ta din na*
> *Kirikita din na*
> *Kirikita din na*
> *TA!*

IRELAND

he *bodhran* (*boh*-rahn) drum goes back in the history of Ireland at least four centuries, if not earlier. A round-frame drum, it is made with goatskin stretched over a wood frame with a crosspiece in the back. In earlier times, the *bodhran* was often used as part of the St. Stephen's Day celebration, which occurs the night after Christmas. In this celebration, also known as the Hunt for the Wren (which probably has its origins in an ancient Druid ceremony), children would go from door to door, asking for money to pay for the burial of a small bird. These processions of children were always accompanied by musicans, dancers, mummers (costumed characters), and *bodhran* players. At the end of the day, the *bodhran*s were destroyed. Today, the use of the *bodhran* has been revived, and the drum has become an important part of many modern Irish folk and popular music ensembles.

The *bodhran* is played, usually, with a stick called a tipper. The tipper stick is held in the hand like a pen and the basic stroke motion is similar to shaking or snapping water off your fingertips. Here is an example of a rhythm that might be played on the *bodhran* to accompany a fast, lively dance called a jig:

County Clare, in the west of Ireland, is the foremost home of traditional music in Ireland today. Every year, a festival is held in the town of Ennistymon (known in Gaelic as Inis Domain) and the surrounding area. People from miles around come to hear and see the best Irish fiddlers, singers, dancers, and *bodhran* players. A *ceilidh* (*kay*-lee) is an all-night party featuring dancing and singing. Food is served and stories are told, people talk about a good ceilidh for days afterward. At the folk music festival in County Clare, ceilidh bands play from morning through night. That is also the time when musicians listen to all kinds of *bodhrans*. Now, many *bodhrans* are made in factories, but in County Clare you can still find *bodhrans* made in the old way. There is a special art to making a *bodhran*. The drum-makers who still practice their craft keep the family secrets closely guarded. The drum-maker will choose a goatskin of just the right strength, just the right thickness, and then bury it in the ground. He might leave it in for one week, or for two or more—that is his own secret. After the skin has been softened in the earth, it will be wrapped around a hoop made from barrel staves. Factory-made *bodhrans* all look the same, but each drum made in the traditional way is unique. It might be perfectly round. Then again, it might be a little bent or oval. And each has its own peculiar tone. At festivals, musicians listen to the sound of the drums they hear. If they like the look or sound of a particular drum, they'll find out who made it, and ask for one of their own from that same drum-maker.

In County Clare there are many legendary musicians, but of all the *bodhran* players and drum-makers, no family is as famous or well known as the Macnamaras. For generations, the Macnamaras have been making and playing the finest *bodhran* drums. In County Clare, it's an accepted fact that wherever the Macnamara brothers, sisters, cousins, aunts, or uncles may be, there will be *bodhran* drums. And of all the Macnamaras, past or present, the greatest player of all was Stevie Macnamara, or Stevie Mac, as he was called. Born at the turn of this century (or even before—nobody knows for sure), Stevie Mac was still playing the drum and mesmerizing his audiences well into old age.

Christy Barry, an Irish musician from County Clare

now living in the United States, told me all about him. He remembers Stevie Mac from his childhood, down to the last detail—the sound of his drum, the sound of his music, his sharp eyes looking out from underneath his thick, craggy eyebrows, the long brown coat he wore summer or winter. For Stevie, drumming was never mechanical. If the occasion was happy, then his rhythms were happy. If he was at a wake, or there was another reason for sadness in the room, his music would reflect that, too. And no violin, concertina, or tin whistle ever sounded so good as when Stevie was there, backing it up with his rhythms. Christy told me, "He played from the heart, for the love of it." His job was to carry on the message of the music, and that's what he did.

bodhran

The Legend of the *Bodhran*

In the old days, you never saw anyone playing the *bodhran* with a stick, the way they do today. A drummer would stretch out his hand from thumb to little finger, and play straight on the drum. You could imagine that after playing all night, drummers' hands would get tired. And indeed they did. But nowadays you'll see most *bodhran* players using a small bone-shaped stick to play the rhythms, and they can keep it up all night long, without ever getting tired. Here's a story of how that all came about. I'm telling it to you in honor of Stevie Mac, the great *bodhran* player of County Clare.

When Stevie Mac was a young man, he lived in a small farmhouse outside his hometown of Inis Domain. But you wouldn't necessarily see his garden weeded or his roof mended, and that's because he was always after playing music. Every day he waited to hear where the nearest wedding or ceilidh was going to be. Then he'd pick up his *bodhran*, whistle a little tune, and set off for wherever that might be. And the people were always glad to see him, because they knew the music never sounded so good as when Stevie Mac was playing along on his *bodhran*.

Stevie Mac liked best of all to play with the concertina, that little accordion that sounds so sweet and haunting. But he was happy to play along with the fiddle or the piano, and especially to play for the dancers. Everyone knew that music wasn't just for listening. Music was for tapping your feet to, and for dancing a jig or a reel. Why, even the old people would get up and step in time when Stevie Mac was beating out the rhythm on the *bodhran*. And no one minded if Stevie Mac's house wasn't the finest, or if his garden wasn't always kept just so, because the music he brought them was worth all the riches in the world.

It happened one time that Stevie had been out playing till the wee hours at the wake of his good old friend, Charlie O'Donnell. Once home, he fell fast asleep, and didn't wake up again till the sun started going down. Stevie jumped out of bed, pulled his brown coat around him (he always wore a brown coat, even in those days), and grabbed his *bodhran*. He was due to play at the Shannon wedding that very night, and here he'd gone and almost slept through it!

He was in such a hurry to get out, he climbed right through the window on the ground floor and over the limb of the tree that leaned across it (Stevie was so busy playing, he didn't always have time to trim the branches, so they grew right through the frames of the house) and rushed off down the road to where he thought the wedding was going to be.

But it was one of those misty, foggy nights in County Clare when it is hard enough to see your hand in front of your face, and there was no moon to speak of. Stevie was in such a rush, he missed the turn to the Shannons' and ended up on one of those lonely little roads leading off the main thoroughfare and into the moors. He followed what he thought was the right path, but soon enough he realized he was in a part of the county he'd never traveled in before. The wind moaned and a soft rain started to fall. Stevie shivered and wrapped his coat tighter around him, with his *bodhran* tucked safely inside.

"It seems I've lost my way," he muttered to himself. "I'd better look for shelter, for it's sure I won't be finding my way back to the village or the Shannon wedding party tonight!" And just as he had that thought, he saw in front of him a wooden bridge that crossed over a narrow stream. Stevie walked across the bridge and found himself looking up a moss-covered hillside, at the top of which stood a large house. The windows were dark. There didn't seem to be a soul in sight. But the rain was turning to a downpour, so he headed toward the iron gates that stood at the bottom of the cobblestone path that led up the hill.

Creeek. The gates were so rusty he could barely get the hinges to move, but move they did, and in a few short minutes he found himself inside the great mansion. It was so dark inside he couldn't see his own hand in front of his face. Stevie felt around in his pocket and found the match and candle he always carried with him in case he needed to tighten the skin of his drum. (*Bodhran* skins aren't fastened with pegs. If the skin is loose, it's best to hold it over the flame of a candle or an open fire till it sounds the right tone again.) Then he looked around.

"All my life I've lived in Inis Domain," he muttered to himself, "and I never saw nor heard of this place." Following the light of the candle, and watching closely the shadows it cast around the room, he walked down a long hallway into what seemed to be an enormous banquet hall or ballroom. At the far end of the hall he could barely make out the shape of a stone fireplace. He walked over to it and sat himself down on a creaky wooden chair in the corner. Outside, the downpour had turned into one of those terrific storms from the Atlantic that sometimes sweep into the west of Ireland. It was cold and damp in the hall, but at least he was indoors. Stevie set his candle down carefully on the floor.

Then he took his *bodhran* out from under his cloak and held it gently over the candle flames, tapping it until it sounded just right. "I won't be playing at a wedding tonight," he said to himself, "but I can play right here, to keep my spirits up!" And he started up with "The Jug of Brown Ale," a cheerful little jig that was one of his favorite tunes. He hummed along to himself, tapping away, when all of a sudden he heard a high-pitched wail echoing through the chimney.

"That's not my voice," he said to himself. "It's not in tune at all with the jig I'm singing. Sure and it's the wind whistling through the walls." And he kept right on playing. He tapped out a few more measures of "The Jug of Brown Ale" and the voice wailed again, this time crying out, "Stevie Mac, if this racket keeps up, I'll be falling through the chimney, and that'll be the end of you!"

But Stevie said to himself, "The song's not over—and besides, nobody tells me when to stop playing. The music stops when it's over!" So he kept right on, and the next time the chorus came around again he heard a whistling sound, and down through the chimney with a *thump* there came the body of a man wearing a sheepskin jacket and leather boots, but nothing around his neck because—he didn't have a head! Stevie didn't blink an eye, because he was coming up to his favorite verse, and the headless man got so caught up in the tune and the rhythms that he hopped up and started to dance the jig right along with Stevie.

The headless man kept dancing, but just then a horrific caterwauling screech echoed down through the same chimney. "Stevie Mac, stop that racket, or I'll fall down the chimney, and that will be the end of you!"

Stevie knew now that the house was haunted by not just one but maybe two ghosts, or more! He was feeling a bit uneasy, and he knew that if he didn't keep on playing, the spirits would do with him as they pleased. So he changed to a reel.

Deedle didle dum, deedle didle dum—fiddle oh!

And sure enough, down through the chimney came a creature with the body of a woman and the head of a goat. But the reel was picking up now, so she began to dance with the headless man, and Stevie just kept on playing. Then he heard another voice echoing in the chimney—this time one with a deep, grumbling growl. "Stevie Mac, stop that *didle dum* infernal racket, or *I'll* be coming down the chimney, and that will surely be the end of you!"

Stevie just whistled another tune, another one of his favorites for all-night parties—a hornpipe this time—and even though his hand was getting a bit tired now, he kept on playing. Down through the chimney with a bump and a crash came a cat with large staring eyes wearing a frock coat and twirling a blackthorn stick as it stood on it hind legs. But it couldn't resist the lively hornpipe music, so it started dancing too, keeping time with its stick as it skipped around the hall. And then, one after the other, down through the chimney came tumbling all the other ghosts and spirits that had been stored up in that house for more years than a man can tell. But Stevie just kept right on playing, from the hornpipe back to the jig and the reel again. And the ghosts and spirits just had to high-step along with Stevie's *bodhran* and whistling.

Finally, just at the point when Stevie thought his hand really would fall off from playing, the stormy night ended and the sun's rays crept over the sky. He looked up for a moment and saw a pale rosy light shimmer through the high windows. When he looked back at the ghosts again, he saw they had all fallen in a heap on the floor, worn out from their wild night of dancing. As more and more light filtered down into the hall, he saw them fading away, one by one, till they had all disappeared into the morning air. Stevie bent down and picked up his candle. It had burned down almost to the end of the wick. He blew it out, put it in his pocket, wrapped his *bodhran* under his coat again, and stood up to go.

"I've missed the wedding," he said to himself, "but what an adventure I've had." Stevie was used to playing for hours at a time, but after *this* night, his hand was tired. His wrist, even his fingers, was numb to the bone. Never had he played so long, so hard, playing for his life, as you might say. As he turned to walk wearily out of the banquet hall, he heard a chorus of whispering voices speaking to him:

"Thanks, Stevie Mac, for the great music of your drum. We haven't had a night of dancing like that since we came into this place. We're the souls that weren't bad enough to go to hell but weren't good enough to go to heaven, either, so we've been stuck in this house for all these many years. Thanks to you, we danced out all our sins, and we danced out all our sorrows. Thanks to you, now we can go on our way to heaven in peace. But next time you play, you might want to give your hand a rest, so we left a gift for you." And there on the floor, in front of the fireplace, he saw a small stick. It was carved of finest wood and shaped just like a bone. An unseen spirit took hold of his hand and placed it gently around the stick, to show him how to strike the skin of his drum just *so*. "Good luck to you and your drumming," the voices said, "and may the gift of the *bodhran* stay with you and your children and your children's children as long as there's music in Ireland!"

When Stevie arrived home, he showed everyone the stick, and told the story of how it came to him. News of it got around, and soon every *bodhran* player from County Clare to Galway was using one. Now they still use a stick called a tipper to play the *bodhran*, and it's all because of Stevie Mac and the night he got lost on the way to the wedding.

GUAJIRO/VENEZUELA

The Guajiro Indians live on a peninsula called La Guajira that juts out into the Caribbean Sea on the border of Venezuela and Colombia. They are one of the largest indigenous groups in the lowlands of South America; they probably originated from deep within the Amazon basin. The Guajira Peninsula is far from a tropical rain forest. The roads and villages are set in a dry, dusty landscape, sprinkled with low-growing bushes and torch cacti. It is here, after a migration that occurred centuries ago, that the Guajiro came to live, establishing a culture that was able to withstand many of the changes wrought by the Europeans who came to Latin America as conquerors, settlers, explorers, and missionaries.

Originally depending on hunting and gathering for their survival, the Guajiro changed when the Spaniards introduced cattle and other livestock into the area. Soon enough, by trading and some expert stealing as well, the Guajiro became better cattle raisers than the Spaniards themselves. In the rainy season they planted corn, cassava, beans, and watermelons. The women, even today, are expert weavers whose hammocks, bags, and shawls are highly prized. Traditional Guajiro families were organized in clans, each one associated with or protected by the spirit of a totem animal, such as the partridge or the jaguar.

Storytelling, festivals, and games were important parts of Guajiro life. In a September harvest festival, amid the feasting and the music, players would divide in two groups in a game called *atkasu palaya suma wuin*—"the sea against the water." Standing back to back, each group—one representing the sea, the other representing the rain—would push against the other. Everyone knew that in the end the waters of the rain, which race to the sea, were always allowed to win!

The *yonna* (yoh-nah) dance was a celebration that could occur anytime—to celebrate a young girl's coming of age, a marriage, or a successful trade. Sometimes spirits would appear in dreams to the Guajiro shaman, demanding that a yonna be held to complete the cure of an ill person or to prevent other calamities that might befall the community. It was at the yonna dance that the drum known as the *kaashi* (*kah*-shee) was played. This drum looked something like a bass drum. Its skin was fastened onto its body by twisted ropes, and it was played with sticks. The music of the *kaashi* accompanied the couples, who danced out a set pattern of steps. The lead dancers and the drummer would often wear headdresses, woven crowns, and armbands made of rooster feathers or the tail of a fox.

Over time much has changed, but traditional beliefs are still important for many Guajiro. Among the most feared spirits in the Guajiro belief system are the evil *wanuluu* (wah-*noo*-loo). In story after story, a wanuluu appears as harbinger of disaster and sorrow. Sometimes, wanuluu appear dressed all in white or black, riding on mules and looking like human beings. At other times they take the shape of animals such as the snake, the fox, or the rabbit. But in every instance, the pierce of a wanuluu arrow can mean nothing but death. In some stories about encounters with the wanuluu, the spirit is victorious and achieves power over his victim, but in many others the hero—be it man, woman, or animal—finds a way to outwit or defeat him.

Today, many young Guajiro have migrated again, this time to the city of Maracaibo in Venezuela or to market towns such as Riohacha, Uribia, and Maicao in Colombia. But the older generation still remember the stories and legends that are the storehouse of their culture and way of life, and the *kaashi* drum still has its place in Guajiro ritual, dance, and myth.

kaashi

Neima's Rescue

Kaliwaa and Neima were brother and sister. They loved each other dearly. Orphaned when very young, they were forced to live with their aunt, a cruel woman who beat and mistreated them day after day. Finally, the two children escaped into the forest. They traveled for many days, but could not find a place that was suitable to be their home. As they walked in the shade of the trees, they came upon four puppies whose mother had been devoured by jaguars. The dogs became their best friends and protectors, and soon after, they found the perfect spot to make their home.

As the two children grew, Kaliwaa became a brave and fearless hunter. Every day he brought home rabbits, deer, and armadillos, which were among the plentiful game of the wood. Neima learned to make all kinds of useful things from the soft clay of the riverbed, fashioning pots, jars, vessels to hold water, and even tubs for washing. They lived happily in the house they had built together. Neima had her own attic, for, as they knew, it would not be proper for them to live together in the same room. And so the days passed on peacefully. The forest was kind to them, and all their needs were satisfied.

Neima became a beautiful young woman. Although they had not seen another soul, either human or spirit, since they had come to the forest, Kaliwaa bade her stay indoors while he was out hunting. "Little sister," he said, "stay inside the house when I'm away, and do not go out or answer anyone who might call you until you see me coming home with the dogs at my side."

Neima promised. And she would have kept her promise. But Yolujaa, the spirit of the dead, had seen the girl once while she was bathing in the river and had fallen desperately in love with her. Although he tried all kinds of tricks, he could not lure her from the house. Finally, in desperation, he called on the help of Chaama, a terrible witch with magic powers who devoured small children and young maidens at every opportunity. When Yolujaa told her of his plight, Chaama was enticed by the thought of the delicious meal Neima would make, and deceitfully agreed to help him. Disguised as a poor old woman, she found her way into Neima's room and enchanted her with stories and legends of the olden times. Her hideous appearance only caused Neima to pity her. When Chaama saw the girl's guard giving way, she invited her to come to her house.

"Oh, no, Grandmother, I couldn't do that," said Neima. "I have promised my brother not to leave. We are very close, and I would not disobey him for the world!"

But Chaama had, among her many powers, the ability to call forth the voices of animals from her head. She caused a rooster to crow, *"Koooo tooo leera kooo!"* and said, "You see, my child, my house is not far. That is the sound of my own rooster you hear!" So Neima agreed to leave with her. No sooner had she stepped out of the house than Chaama spirited her away, preparing to eat her.

Kaliwaa returned home, and finding his sister gone, he went in desperate search of her with his dogs at his side. The little *chuuta* bird helped him, and the next day Kaliwaa found the place where Chaama lived. Neima had been cut up into tiny pieces, which hung on the branches of a nearby tree. In fury, Kaliwaa set his dogs on the witch. Though she tried to escape, the dogs were too powerful for her, their sharp teeth digging into her flesh. Crying out for mercy, Chaama promised to bring Neima back to life if the dogs would let her go. After Kaliwaa had called them off, Chaama gathered all the pieces of the young girl and put them in a pot of boiling water. Within minutes, the parts of the body were joined together again. Neima stepped out, fresh and young, beautiful as ever.

"What a strange sleep I have had," she said. "I must have had a nightmare!" Kaliwaa took one more look at Chaama and then, in revenge, gave her a blow on the head with his club. The rooster, the hens, and the dogs that had lived inside there— cackling and crowing, barking and squeaking—flew off and disappeared. He hadn't killed her, but from that day on Chaama's power was destroyed forever.

On their way home, at a place where two paths crossed, Kaliwaa and Neima saw someone riding on the back of a fox. He was dressed all in white. His hat seemed to shine, as did the rings that he wore. It was a wanuluu—an evil spirit of the forest. As soon as the dogs saw him, they growled and attacked, almost knocking him to the ground. The wanuluu brushed himself off and said to Kaliwaa, "Your dogs have injured me! I demand payment for this insult!"

"My dogs are used to chasing foxes, that is all," replied the young man, unafraid. "Besides, I have nothing to pay you with."

"Then give me that young girl who is riding beside you. She will be payment enough."

Kaliwaa laughed. "You must think I'm a fool indeed, to part with my beloved sister. Be off now, I'm
warning you!" And with that he set his dogs on the
wanuluu in earnest. But the wanuluu had great powers himself. With his mighty hands he ground the
dogs into dust. They blew away into the wind, and
never returned again. As for Neima, the wanuluu
picked her up as easily as a feather and carried her
off with him on the back of his fox.

Kaliwaa wept and wept. He returned home, but
could not think of what to do next. The house fell
into decay. The garden withered. And just when it
seemed that all was lost, he was visited one day by
Molokoona, the turtle. Molokoona the master
drummer.

"My friend, I have seen you weeping here now,
day after day. I am only a humble turtle, with a
hard-backed shell and a wrinkled face, but I think I
can help you. I think I can be the one to find your
sister, and I won't rest until I succeed." And with
that, he set off on his way.

For days Molokoona traveled. For weeks and
months he fought his way across rivers and through
the underbrush, and finally, when he had almost
given up hope, he came to a place where he heard
voices laughing and shouting. It was a party. A party
of spirits. He had reached the house of the wanuluu.
Now, in those days, wherever Molokoona went, he
brought his drumsticks with him, tied in a pouch

NEIMA'S RESCUE • 97

that he carried on his back, for he never knew when
he would be invited to play the *kaashi* for a festival
or a yonna dance. For miles around he was known
for his drumming skill, and no one was called upon
to play as often as he.

Molokoona entered the house where the party
was taking place. All around were spirits, drinking
and guzzling, clamoring and guffawing. Loudest of
them all was the wanuluu.

"So, newcomer—I see by the pouch on your scaly
back that you are a drummer! Are you any good?"

"That is what the people say," replied Molokoona
in a soft voice.

"Ho! If that is so, play for us now, or you won't
leave here alive!"

Molokoona calmly agreed and strapped the *kaashi*
drum of the house around his hard shell.

"No, wait, don't start yet!" called out the wanuluu.
"First, a drink!" The wanuluu planned to make him
so drunk that he wouldn't be able to play. Then he
and his friends could beat him to a pulp before they
kicked him out into the forest to die.

Molokoona was clever. He took the rum they offered him, but instead of pouring the liquor down
his gullet, he poured it down his neck, behind the
collar of his shirt. The hot liquor burned him, and
that is why, to this day, the turtle's neck is wrinkled,
but on that day Molokoona didn't say a thing. He
gritted his teeth and kept quiet. Then he started to

play. With slow, unsteady beats, he started and stopped, started and stopped.

"You should be able to do better than that, or your end will come sooner than you think!" roared the wanuluu. "Here, have another drink!"

Again Molokoona poured the rum down his shirt. When he picked up the sticks again, he played as he always did. With strength and power the rhythms of the *kaashi* sounded out into the night. The spirits stopped their carousing and listened. "You do play well," cackled the wanuluu. "Here, take a gourd of rum." Again Molokoona only pretended to drink, but the crowd around him was impressed. They'd never heard such a good drummer, and they had never seen anyone who could swallow so much rum without getting drunk in the bargain!

Molokoona played on. The guests beat their fists on the tables and chairs, and chanted along in between gulps of drink and gobbles of food. Finally Molokoona said, "I see you have a nice large kitchen. I'd like to go in there and tune up my drum."

"Go right ahead," roared the wanuluu. "But make it quick, I'm enjoying the music!"

Molokoona kept on beating the drum quietly, but when he got into the kitchen, he saw Neima, who sat huddled in misery by the fire. "Hurry up, girl, and get inside my drum! I'm going to save you from this prison and bring you back to your brother! Just remember to hold your ears once you're inside, or you'll go deaf!" And with that Neima crept into the drum, holding her ears for dear life.

"What's taking you so long?" shouted the wanuluu.

"I'm lighting my cigar!" Molokoona replied casually. Then he picked up the drum with Neima inside and made his way toward the door, beating it as he went along.

"That drum doesn't sound anymore!" growled the wanuluu. "The party's over!" And in a huff he sent everyone away. Molokoona kept on beating the drum quietly as he crossed over the threshold and set off into the bush. Meanwhile, the wanuluu went into the kitchen to look for Neima. Seeing the girl gone, he flew into a rage. "Someone's stolen my wife! It was that turtle who tricked me with his cigars and his drumming!" And he set off after him.

Molokoona hadn't gone far, for the drum was heavy with Neima still hidden inside, and soon enough the wanuluu caught up with them.

"What have you done with my wife, you miserable crack-shelled thief!"

"I don't have the slightest idea what you're talking about," the turtle replied in his nonchalant way. "I've never even seen your wife."

"Give her back!" yelled the wanuluu as he slashed at the turtle with his whip.

But Molokoona easily turned it aside with his drumsticks, twisting the cord around them with his wrists and flipping the wanuluu over his shoulder. *Crash!* The wanuluu fell to the ground. He scrambled up and charged at Molokoona again, brandishing his spear, but Molokoona calmly held out his drumsticks and poked the evil spirit in the eyes as he rushed toward him, blinding him with one stroke. Screaming in pain and anger, the wanuluu held his hands to his useless eyes and stumbled off. Blinded and lost in the forest, he was never seen or heard of again.

Neima jumped out of the drum and thanked Molokoona profusely. "Let's go home now!" she cried. After many days of travel, they returned to Kaliwaa in a triumphant procession, with Molokoona beating on the *kaashi* with rolls and trills, and Neima skipping joyfully beside him.

When they returned home, many other adventures awaited the faithful pair—some happy, others sad. To this day, Kaliwaa is remembered by a sweet wild plant that grows along twisting paths and roadsides, and Neima by the river on the Guajira Peninsula that carries her name.

AZTEC/MEXICO

epoztlán is an ancient town surrounded by high cliffs and mountains, about sixty miles south of Mexico City. Most of the people of Tepoztlán are descendants of the Aztec civilization that once held sway over most of Mexico, before the Spanish conquest by Cortés and his army in 1521. Even today, two languages are spoken there—the Spanish brought to Mexico by the conquistadors and the missionaries, and Nahuatl, the indigenous language of Aztec origin that has survived into the twentieth century. The air of Tepoztlán is dry and crisp. Many of the streets in this hillside town are paved and terraced according to the old Aztec system, but Spanish-style houses, too, border the town square.

Life in Tepoztlán revolves around planting corn and other crops. People often travel the mountain roads on burros or wagons pulled by oxen. Their calendar is marked by a year-long cycle of religious observances and celebrations based on themes and symbols of the Catholic Church. But many earlier beliefs and customs have survived, gradually mixing in with church rituals and observances. One of the oldest celebrations in Tepoztlán, and one that is still observed today, is *La Fiesta de la Virgen de la Natividad*—the Festival of the Virgin of the Nativity. This festival, which takes place on September 8, honors Tepozteco.

According to tradition, Tepozteco was a real king who lived during the time of the Toltecs whose civilization flourished in the region and was eventually absorbed, through war and battle, by the Aztecs. As time passed, the legends and stories of his exploits grew, until finally he was worshiped as a god. One of these legends is recounted in the town square of Tepoztlán during the September festival, with townspeople acting out the roles of Tepozteco and the kings who battled against him. In the myth of his birth, Tepozteco's mother was portrayed as a virgin, impregnated by a seed she ate while cleaning the holy temple of Ometochtli. Later, as a Catholic symbol, she gave her name—la Virgen de la Natividad—to the yearly celebration.

It is only once a year, during this festival, that the *teponaztli* (teh-poh-*nahz*—t'lee)—the sacred drum of Tepozteco—is brought out from the sacristy of the town church and played for all the people to hear. The *teponaztli* itself is a small, carved, double-slitted drum that is struck with wooden mallets. By striking the various tones of the drum, the musician can create melodious rhythmic patterns to accompany the speeches and dialogues that are performed by the actors. Here is an example of a simple *teponaztli* rhythm:

Tepozteco is still important to the villagers. Children learn that the god lives in a house on a mountaintop, far above the clouds. If the villagers give him a good celebration on September 8, he is content. But if he is displeased, he can send down *los aires*—mysterious spirits carried on the wind who bring diseases and misfortune. The worship of Tepozteco began many centuries ago, but some still believe that he can appear to his people in times of need.

The legend of Tepozteco, sung and reenacted every year to the ringing accompaniment of the *teponaztli* drum, is a way for all the people of Tepoztlán to remember and celebrate their proud and ancient history.

teponaztli

The Feast for Tepozteco

📿 📿 📿 Long ago, a great temple to the god Ometochtli stood on a mountaintop near Tepoztlán. Every day, young maidens of the valley below would climb the steep hillside to tend the temple grounds. One day, while sweeping the floor near the altar, one of the young women found a small seed caught in a crevice between two stones. Curious to see how it would taste, she put it in her mouth, and then swallowed it.

Soon after, the young maiden found that she was pregnant, and within a year she gave birth to a child, a baby boy. But the girl was ashamed of what had happened. She wanted to keep it a secret. So she took the baby and left him at the foot of the cliffs of Atongo, which stood by the river that flowed east of the town.

The next day, an old couple came to the stream to wash their clothes and found the baby, still alive, nestled in the weeds by the riverbed. They picked him up out of the water, wrapped him in a warm blanket, took him home to their cane-covered hut, and raised him as their own son. The old couple, who had never had any children, looked after the child they had found with love and care. They called him Tepozteco.

Now at that time there was a terrible monster named Xochicalcatl who tyrannized the people of the valley. Every day he demanded that one older person be delivered to him for his daily meal. The monster lived to the east of the valley, in a place called Xochicalco, and every day someone was chosen to make the journey there to meet this sad fate. When Tepozteco was ten years old, there came a day when his own father was chosen to be the next victim.

"Father," said Tepozteco, "let me go in your place."

The old man refused. "My son," he said, "I have already lived long enough. You are just a young boy, small and weak. Even if you were to sacrifice yourself, Xochicalcatl would never be satisfied, and then who knows what vengeance he would wreak on our town and our people. It is better that I go now."

But the boy insisted, and finally, with great sadness in their hearts, the old couple let him go. Before he left, Tepozteco told them to watch the skies in the east, and if they saw a white cloud rising, it would mean that he had succeeded in vanquishing the monster. If the cloud was black, it would mean that he, too, had met his end at the hands of Xochicalcatl. With many tears and prayers for his safety, the couple bade farewell to their beloved child.

As he journeyed to the east to meet the monster, Tepozteco picked up pieces of sharp obsidian that he found by the roadside and put them in the pack he carried around his waist. When he reached Xochicalco, he called out to the monster: "I am your offering today. Come and find me! I am ready to stand before you!"

The monster looked at him disdainfully. "The people of the valley have become foolish indeed, to send such a small creature as you for my daily meal. Why, I can swallow you with one gulp, and eat a dozen more of you! Be off with you, and send someone of the right size, or I will destroy the people of the valley!"

Tepozteco stood firm. He did not move from his spot. And Xochicalçatl, being hungry and greedy as ever, finally gave in. He kept to his word and swallowed the boy with one gulp, without even chewing him.

Tepozteco found himself inside the belly of the monster. It was cold and very dark. But he was alive. He took out the pieces of sharp stone he had collected and began to slice away at the monster's flesh. Soon he pierced a hole right through the tough skin, and he emerged safe and sound. Xochicalcatl lay dead, mortally wounded from the sharp gashes of the obsidian. Tepozteco had saved his father and all the people of the valley, and as he set off for home, the old couple, who had been watching the sky anxiously, saw a luminous white cloud floating up into the east.

Years passed, and Tepozteco became king, known throughout the valley for his bravery, strength, and wisdom. Wherever he went, he was accompanied by a drummer playing the *teponaztli*, the melodious royal drum, and another musician who struck the *sonaja* (soh-*nah*-ha)—the ringing bell that announced his arrival. Tales of his magic powers and miraculous feats spread far and wide. One day Tepozteco received an invitation from four neighboring kings to attend a feast they were giving and join their royal council. Tepozteco gladly accepted their offer, for both he and his people desired peace with the surrounding kingdoms.

The day of the feast arrived. The kings of Yautepec, Huaxtepec, Tlayacapa, and Cuahnahuac were seated with their vassals and followers in their great banquet hall. The tables were set with sumptuous food. It seemed as if the gods themselves were gathered there, so magnificent were the royal garments of the kings and their guests. From the courtyard outside, a sound was heard. It was the beating of the *teponaztli* and the silver chimes of the bell. Tepozteco had arrived! The kings and all their guests stood up expectantly to greet him. Long had they heard of his prowess and his deeds. Now they were going to meet this already legendary ruler. The sound of the drum grew louder, the bell echoed through the hall, and finally Tepozteco appeared. The mouths of the kings and their guests dropped open. For there stood a young man, dressed in simple clothing, with nothing but sandals to cover his bare feet and a woven white cloth draped over his shoulders.

"Greetings," he said simply. "I am honored to be part of this royal gathering."

King Cuahnahuac drew himself up haughtily. "Tepozteco, we have invited you to this banquet thinking we would meet a person of royal bearing like ourselves. Instead, you come dressed in these peasant clothes, with no one but your musicians to follow you! Your appearance is an insult to yourself and all the great kings and counselors who have come here today. There is no place for you here!" And so saying, he and all the other kings sat down, and motioned their followers to do the same.

Tepozteco smiled ruefully and replied, "Then I will return in the manner which you see fit." He disappeared out of the palace, and in a short time he returned. Once again, the *teponaztli* and the bell announced his arrival. This time he was dressed in the most magnificent clothing. A royal mantle, shining with gold and jewels, hung around his shoulders. He was crowned with a headdress of the most brilliant feathers, the red and gold of the quetzal bird itself. In his hands he carried a shield studded with jade and obsidian, and bands of turquoise circled his wrists and arms.

"Now you may sit with us!" The four kings nodded approvingly. "Let the feast begin!"

But as soon as he sat down, Tepozteco began to do a very strange thing. He took off his mantle and crown and placed them beside him. As the plates of food and drink were passed around, he poured everything onto the royal cape and headdress.

"What strange behavior is this?" the king of Tlayacapa said. "Are you mocking our feast?"

"Not in the slightest," replied Tepozteco coolly. "But from your first greeting, I understood that it was not me you were interested in inviting to this sumptuous occasion—it was my royal garments. And so it is only right that they should receive the bounty you are offering here today."

The four kings rose up in fury. "You have mocked us!" they cried. "That is no way to speak to your fellow kings!" And with that they set upon Tepozteco, ordering their soldiers to chase and overcome him. Tepozteco fled. His musicians followed closely behind. He knew he had little chance to defend himself, without even a spear at hand. The king's soldiers pursued him, but Tepozteco was faster. He reached the top of La Montana del Aire—the Mountain of the Air—where his people had already built a great temple for him. There he stood, with the *teponaztli* beating out the sounds of war and battle. He lifted up his arms and the ground began to quake. As the earth shook, a barricade of cliffs suddenly appeared, blocking the way to the mountain. He shot out his hands and thunder and lightning pierced the sky. The soldiers were confused and terrified. They could not reach him. Tepozteco taunted them, while the *teponaztli* echoed his every word and the bell chimed in, reverberating down the mountainside.

Tepozteco never again returned to earth as king. He remains forever in the mountain of the clouds. But he still watches over and protects his people, the people of Tepoztlán. And as a sign of his everlasting love and kingship he left a gift for them, a gift that to this day is guarded safely in the sacristy of La Santísima Church. It is heard only once a year, when the townsfolk gather to honor his name and tell his story—the gift of his sacred drum, the royal *teponaztli*.

JEWISH/BIBLICAL LEGEND

rums of all kinds and varieties have long played a part in the music and ritual of Middle Eastern peoples. A multitude of drums and percussive styles can be found from Yemen to Morocco, from the Sudan to Israel, from Iran to Syria. One of the most widespread instruments is the goblet-shaped drum known in the Arabic-speaking world as the *dumbek*, *darbukka*, or *tabl*. In Iran it is known as the *zarb* and in Israel as the *tof*. Other kinds of hand percussion instruments are played throughout the Middle East as well. Frame drums, such as the *tar* or *bendir*, are particularly popular in much of the region. Through archaeological remains we know that such drums, as well as other instruments, existed in the ancient kingdoms of Egypt, Sumeria, Babylonia, and Mesopotamia. Often it was the women who played them as part of temple rituals in service to the gods.

In ancient Israel, too, women played these instruments to accompany dancing at festivities and religious ceremonies. The most common of these drums was the timbrel, a small round-frame drum hung with bells. The Book of Exodus (15:20) says: "And Miriam the prophetess, the sister of Aaron, took a timbrel in her hand; and all the women went out after her with timbrels and with dances. And Miriam sung unto them. . . ." The Hebrew word *tof*, for "drum," is mentioned fifteen times in the Torah (the first five books of the Bible) and is still used today.

Master drummers, whether men or women, use their fingers almost the way a pianist does, creating many high and deep tones with fast finger movements, snaps, and trills. As with many of the drums in this book, there are Middle Eastern drum syllables, such as *dum* for the deep low tone, created by striking the center of the drum with an open hand, and *tak*, created with a sharp snapping or tapping on the edge of the drum. There are many musical phrases and combinations of beats in Middle Eastern playing. One of the phrases played on the goblet-shaped *dumbek* is a pattern that looks like this:

Here is another rhythm, called *duyek*, that is played on the Turkish *bendir*, the frame drum:

dum   te   ke   tek   kya   du   me   dum   tek

Perhaps these rhythms were played centuries ago, in the times when the Hebrews, Egyptians, and other early peoples mingled together in the deserts and wadis, caravan trails, small towns, and great cities of Near Eastern civilization. They can be heard today in the Israeli *hora*, the Arab *debka*, and countless other songs and dances that are still a vibrant part of Middle Eastern life and culture.

dumbek

Miriam at the Red Sea

Miriam sat with her head in her hands. For days now, she had seen the divine punishments fall on the heads of the Egyptians. Darkness had covered the land. The Nile had turned red with blood. Locusts and hail had fallen on the fields, but still Pharaoh had refused to heed the pleas of her people. Still he had refused to let them go free.

Finally, the most terrible plague of all had befallen the land. The angel of death had passed over the houses of the Israelites and had smitten the firstborn sons of the Egyptians. Pharaoh's son himself had been taken. But still, deep into the night, no one knew what was to happen next. All of a sudden, Miriam heard the piercing blast of the *shofar* (*show-far*) and the echoes of running feet as the messengers ran over the narrow stone streets of Goshen. "It is time to go now! Moses has said it. Pharaoh has let us go. We must hurry. There is no time to lose. Bring only one thing with you, something you can carry on your back through the desert. It's time to go!"

Miriam looked hurriedly around the darkened room. What to bring on this long journey? And then her eyes lit on her most precious possession, the thing she valued above all others. It was her little *tof*, the clay drum that she played to accompany the songs and dances that had brought her people some moments of happiness throughout the long years of captivity. She treasured this little drum. Quickly she tied a measure of twine on either end, so that she could carry it easily over her shoulder.

Then she wrapped a shawl over her head and ran out into the night.

All the people had gathered behind Moses and Aaron, jostling and pushing. Miriam ran through the crowd and stood at her brother's side. "I was waiting for you," Moses said. "It's time to go." Out of Goshen they fled, across the fields, beyond the boundaries of Pharaoh's kingdom, and into the desert. Miriam turned around and looked one last time at the place that had always been her home—the tumbledown shacks, the muddy streets, the rank water, and the endless, endless piles of brick, stone, and mortar that ruled every waking moment of their lives. To all this she said good-bye. But even as she left, her heart tugged at her too, for this hard and rugged place was still the only home she had ever known.

Into the night they sped, and when dawn reached out over the horizon, the city of Pharaoh was far behind them. Children cried on their mothers' backs. Old men and women struggled to keep up, helped by their younger sons and daughters. The sun rose higher. Its heat seemed to beat down on their heads as the grasslands and marshes of the Nile Valley turned to dry dust and sand. The desert was upon them. Suddenly, a scout in the rear guard called out, "There's a cloud of dust in the distance. Horsemen are coming! Pharaoh has changed his mind. The soldiers are coming after us!"

Confusion and fear rose in the people's hearts. "Moses," they called out. "Moses, help us. You've brought us out here by God's command. Now are we all to die?"

Moses turned and gazed across the sand. He saw the rolling dust coming closer and closer. "We're not stopping," he said. "We are going on!" And on they went. Miriam ran on, holding the drum tightly against her.

In the distance, a strange swirling sound broke the desert silence. "It's the sea!" the scouts called out. "It's the sea. We've reached the shores of the Red Sea!"

Tumbling and pushing, the people followed the scouts. Led by Moses and Aaron, they kept going until they stood by the churning waters. "We cannot cross!" wept an old man. "We cannot cross and Pharaoh's soldiers are coming! Where is God now? We are lost!" "We're lost," cried the people. "We are lost. Let us surrender now while there is still time!" Moses and Aaron pleaded for calm, but panic swept through the crowd.

At that moment they heard a sound. It was a familiar sound, the sound that had given them joy and raised their spirits, even through the years of enslavement and toil. "Once we were slaves," Miriam sang out, "and now we're going to be free!" One by one they turned to her. Miriam stood firm, gazing into their faces as her nimble fingers called out the deep and high tones of the little clay drum.

"Once we were slaves," the people began to sing with her, "and now we are going to be free!"

The drum rang out. Miriam played on, strong and clear. Moses raised his staff, and as their voices lifted even higher, the waters of the sea drew apart, and a path of dry land emerged in the rushing waves. "Who will follow me?" cried out Miriam. "Who will follow my brother Moses across the waters?"

One by one, the people—the old men, the women, the young children—followed Moses into the parting waters. Miriam stood on the shore urging them on, playing out the call of the drum, as Pharaoh's army came closer and closer. She was the last to go across. As she dashed into the sea, the waves towered above her head. She carried her drum high, lifting it up so that everyone who had already reached the shore could see it. Like walls, the waters rose on either side of her. At last she stepped onto dry land. All the people were gathered there, gazing and pointing back toward the waves they had just passed through.

Miriam turned to see what they were looking at. The chariots of Pharaoh had rushed into the sea after them. She could see the swords of the soldiers, and their blades glinting in the sun. And then, as if by a silent signal known only to them, the waters closed. The path disappeared and the soldiers, their horses, their chariots, and their weapons were carried away and into the roiling waters. Miriam held her drum close. She almost sang out again—but she seemed to hear a voice, a voice that was still and small. A voice that was far away, yet close within her. And the voice said, "How can you sing in praise when my children are drowning?"

Miriam stopped. All the people were quiet. Even the angels in heaven, it seemed, were silent as the people stood with heads bowed. Then, together, they lifted their heads and gazed at one another in joy and thankfulness. They looked to Miriam, and with trembling hands she lifted the drum to her shoulder and began to play again, as the people shouted and danced. "Once we were slaves. And now we *are* free!"

Miriam traveled with her people for their many years of wandering in the wilderness. Troubles and hardships beset them, but they never lost hope. Through all the hardships, Miriam's song and music gave her people courage. After her death the drum disappeared, and no one has been able to find it, but the memory of its sounds echoes through the generations, renewing its voice every year at the celebration of Passover. Even today, the clay drum is called in Hebrew *tof Miriam* in honor of the prophetess, dancer, and drummer who helped lead her people to freedom.

Epilogue

🦋 🦋 🦋

One spring afternoon not too long ago, I went to see a master drummer from Nigeria who was visiting New York City for a short time. The drummer's name is Adeleke Sangoyoyin, which means "Shango brings honey." He travels around the world teaching the art, music, and traditions of Yoruba culture. As I sat with him, his host translating when needed, Adeleke told me of how he grew up on a farm in the countryside. He recalled learning the craft of carving from his grandfather in between classes at the local school, and how he became a master drummer by watching and joining in with the musicians who played at parties and celebrations in his town, Iragbiji.

There were many drums crowded into the small apartment. Several Nigerian talking drums, called *dundun* (doon-doon), hung with bells and covered tightly with twine, were gathered in one corner. On a piece of beautifully dyed batik cloth that Adeleke had made was the small, round, kettle-shaped drum called *gudugudu* (goo-doo-goo-doo)—the first drum he had played as a child.

As we sat, he sang an orisha chant for me, and told me the story of Ayan, god of the drums. Adeleke told me that long ago the god Ayan went to spend some time in the house of Olorun, the ruler and sky god. He listened there to all the conversations among the other visitors—the leaves, the water, and the wind. When he returned to his own home, Ayan wanted to remember all the wonderful things he had heard, so he made a small wooden drum—the *gudugudu*—in his own image. Ayan made the drum so that all the stories that were told at the beginning of the world could be remembered and passed on in a language that all could understand.

Adeleke told me that when he was a young boy, his father gave him his own small drum and told him to choose a special place in the forest, and to go there and play all the sounds that he heard. When he returned, his father listened to his rhythms and stroked him on the head, saying, "Good, good." At first, Adeleke said, he did not understand what his father had wanted him to do, but later he remembered how hard he had listened to the sounds around him and, by playing them back, how much he had learned about concentrating and communicating.

You too can find a special place, whether it's on a busy city street or by a forest stream. Listen to the conversations you hear, then find yourself a drum, your own drum, and create the sounds you heard. Then share them with others. In this way you become part of a great tradition, adding your voice, your language, your stories, to the world of rhythms that have soothed and rocked, enthralled and inspired, the hearts of all peoples in all places in all times.

At the end of my meeting with Adeleke, he said to me, "May the spirit of Ayan always be with you."

And so may it be with you.

gudugudu

Explanatory Notes

♯ ♯ ♯

Instrument Terminology

In 1914, Erich Von Hornbostsel and Curt Sachs developed a system of classifications for musical instruments that is still used today by ethnomusicologists (scholars who study musical instruments and music's role in culture) and music educators. They based their categories on a system of instrument classification that had already been developed by scholars of ancient India, in which the method of sound production identified instrument groupings. The four main categories, which can be applied to instruments all over the world, are *aerophones* (sound is made by blowing), *chordophones* (sound is made by plucking or bowing a string), *membranophones* (sound is made by striking an object covered with skin), and *idiophones* (sound is made from shaking, striking, scraping, etc., the material itself). The drums in this book fall into either the membranophone or the idiophone category. For example, the *lali* drum and the *teponaztli* are idiophones, while the *tabla, bodhran,* and *changgo* are membranophones, because the sound they make is created when their skin is struck.

Types of Drums

According to ethnomusicologists, there are several basic types of drum shapes. Each of these shapes has many variations found all over the globe. Here is a list of these shapes and how the drums mentioned in this book fall into the basic categories:

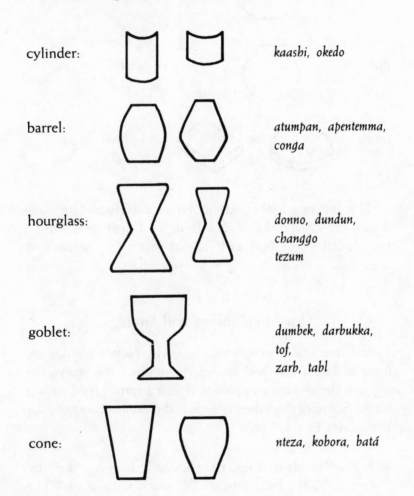

cylinder: *kaashi, okedo*

barrel: *atumpan, apentemma, conga*

hourglass: *donno, dundun, changgo tezum*

goblet: *dumbek, darbukka, tof, zarb, tabl*

cone: *nteza, kobora, batá*

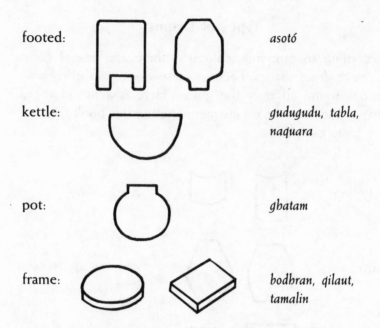

footed: *asotó*

kettle: *gudugudu, tabla, naquara*

pot: *ghatam*

frame: *bodhran, qilaut, tamalin*

The information on drum types described here was drawn from *Music of the Whole Earth,* by David Reck, which is included in the Further Readings section at the back of the book.

Story Beginnings and Endings

In oral traditions throughout the world, certain phrases are used to begin and end stories. Sometimes the storyteller will ask the audience to join in before beginning or ending a tale. Some of these beginnings and endings were used for the stories in this book:

Krik! Krak! In Haiti, a teller traditionally begins a story by saying *"Krik!"* The audience responds with *"Krak!"* The storyteller can use this call-and-response signal at any time during the telling.

"We do not mean, we do not really mean, that everything you're about to hear is the truth" is the translation of a traditional story beginning from West Africa.

Yennal yennal-é are the Korean words for "long, long ago," or "in old times."

batá

Glossary

apsara: celestial dancers of Hindu mythology, who live in the royal palace of the god Indra.

Bhashmashur: In Sanskrit, *bhashma* means "ash," and *asura*, "demon." Thus, the name of the character in the story, Bhashmashur, means "ash-demon."

Dravidian: refers to the languages, such as Tamil and Telugu, as well as to the people of southern India who are descendants of pre-Aryan civilization that once dominated the Indus Valley.

Druid: the priest, teacher, or diviner of Celtic culture who presided over rituals and ceremonies.

Gaelic: the language spoken by the Celts, the people who inhabited the British Isles before the Roman Empire and the rise of Christianity. Varieties of Gaelic are still studied and spoken in parts of Ireland, the Isle of Man, and Scotland today.

gandarva: celestial musicans of Hindu mythology, who live with the apsaras in the royal palace of the god Indra. In India when musicians play, it is a custom to burn incense, in the belief that the sweet scent will attract the presence of the gandarvas.

haegol: Korean word for skull, skeleton, or bones.

Mt. Khailash: a mountain of the northern Himalayas in what is now Chinese-occupied Tibet, close to the borders of India and China, northwest of Nepal. It is still considered a holy site, which people on pilgrimages visit throughout the year.

quetzal: a Central American bird with brilliant plumage. *Quetzalcoatl*, the plumed serpent god, was an important deity in Aztec mythology.

Sanskrit: the classical language of the Hindu scripture of ancient India.

shaman: a term for the person who in many traditional cultures acts as the priest, the doctor, and the storyteller. Shamans are particularly trained in communication with the spirit world to aid the fellow members of their community. In some cultures, such as the Inuit, only men can be shamans. In others, such as in Korea or among the Guajiro, the shaman will often be a woman.

Shango: in the Yoruba pantheon, Shango is one of the *orisha*, a god who is associated with the powers of thunder and lightning. He is also owner of the sacred drums called *batá*.

shofar: a ram's horn used by the ancient Israelites to sound an alarm and announce important events. It is still played today in synagogue rituals on high holy days.

sombo: the word for "alas" in Fiji.

Sufi: a member of a mystical sect of Islam that originated in Persia.

tala: This word for rhythmic cycles is actually a combination of two other Sanskrit words: *tandarva* is used to describe the male aspect of dance styles; *lasia* is the female aspect of classical dance.

About the Stories

𝅘𝅥 𝅘𝅥 𝅘𝅥

Introduction

Louis Bauzo, director of the Latin Music Program at the Harbor Performing Arts Center in New York City and my Latin percussion teacher for many years, was the one who first explained the word *patakín* to me. *Patakín* is also the name of his Afro–Cuban dance and drumming group, which performs throughout New York City and nationally. A definition for the word can be found in Lydia Cabrera's classic dictionary of Afro–Cuban terms, *Anagó: Vocabulario Lucumí*. I wish to thank ethnomusicologist Morty Marks for referring me to this book.

Skeleton Woman

I first heard this story in 1976 from a wonderful storyteller and pioneering dance therapist, the late Mara Capy. I soon began to retell and perform it in schools, museums, and senior-citizen centers. I later discovered it in a written version in Maurice Metayer's collection *Tales from the Igloo*, under the title "The Magic Drum." The information on Inuit drumming was culled from various sources, including the wonderful book *Learning Eskimo Drumming*, by Thomas F.

Johnston and Tupou Pulu, and the Folkways recording *Eskimos of Hudson Bay and Alaska*. The original saying "To stop the Eskimo from singing and dancing is like cutting the tongue out of a bird" is included in Laura Boulton's liner notes to the Folkways album. It was told to her by an elderly Alaska native woman during the 1920s when the recording was first made. I'm also grateful to the faculty members of the Alaska Native Languages Center at the University of Alaska at Fairbanks for reviewing the story.

The Elephant King's Drum

This retelling is adapted from Harold Courlander's tale "Merisier, Stronger Than the Elephants," in *The Piece of Fire and Other Haitian Tales*, which he collected and transcribed from a Haitian storyteller. Merisier, the priest in the story, is the name of an actual historical figure, a powerful priest of vodou who played a significant role in political conflicts that occurred in Haiti in the late nineteenth century. You can read more about him and many aspects of Haitian culture in Courlander's book *The Drum and the Hoe: Life and Lore of the Haitian People*. For the purpose of this book some changes were made to Courlander's version. I incorporated the *asotó* drum and the *ason* rattle, because I wanted to use names of instruments that are still played today in Haiti. The location of the farmer's home in Fort-Liberté, as well as the names of the other sons and my description of the mapou tree, were also added elements, gathered from interviews with scholars as well as Haitians living in New York. Gage Averill, professor of ethnomusicology at Wesleyan University, gave me invaluable background information on Haitian culture and drumming, as did Richard Hill, master teacher of West African and Caribbean drumming traditions and the director of the African/Caribbean group

Mikata. I am also grateful to Frisner Augustin, a Haitian master drummer living in New York City and the director of *Troupe Makandal,* who taught me to play kongo rhythms and reviewed the story with me for accuracy and detail.

Anansi and the Secret Name

This story was adapted from the Ashanti tale "Sky God's Daughter," which appears in Harold Courlander's collection *The King's Drum and Other African Stories.* In the process of re-creating the story for this book, I consulted with one of my drumming teachers, Ghanaian master drummer Abraham Kobena Adzenyah, adjunct professor on the faculty of Wesleyan University's World Music Program. Some of the changes to the original are the result of those conversations. In Courlander's version, it is Nyame, the Sky God, who is the chief and father of Beduasemanpensa. Nyame does appear in many Ashanti folktales, and more recently has even been depicted in picture books of some of these tales. However, in Ghana, he is mostly perceived as an "unseen" god, the highest of all deities in Akan religion. Therefore, I chose to portray the chief as a human character, and gave him a name suggested by Abraham Adzenyah—Otuakenten. The interpolations of drum poetry were also generously provided to me by Abraham from his 1978 master's thesis, "Acquisition of Musical Knowledge by Traditional Musicians of the Akan Society: A Study of Akan Music Education." Transcriptions of drum poetry can also be found in the books of J. H. Kwabena Nketia, Ghana's foremost ethnomusicologist. For the purposes of this book, I also included names of actual Akan drums, such as the *donno, atumpan, fontomfrom,* and *apentemma.* In "Sky God's Daughter," Courlander's ending does not in-

clude a reference to the origin of any particular character-
istic of the lizard. However, this turn of plot does occur in
another variant of this story, "Why the Lizard Stretches
His Neck," by Peggy Appiah in her collection *Anansi the
Spider: Tales from an Ashanti Village*. In discussing various aspects of Nyame, Abraham Adzenyah also related a myth
to me in which Nyame "reached down" and blessed a crippled girl, giving her an arm made of gold. For this version, we both thought it would be an appropriate ending
for Nyame to "bless" the lizard (*Abosom-kitsu* means
"chameleon" in Twi) in a similar way, by giving him the
ability to change colors and thus escape Anansi. Finally,
Courlander's version ends with a proverb, an authentic
feature of much Ashanti storytelling whereas I use the traditional story ending. "Anansi and the Secret Name," therefore, is a composite tale drawing on various sources, all of
which are based on Akan beliefs and cultural practices. I
recommend Harold Courlander's version for further read-
ing. Musician and scholar Richard Hill was also of tremendous help in sharing his knowledge of Ghanaian drumming
and cultural traditions during my research for the story.

The Silent Drum of Ono Island

I first encountered this story, titled "The Drum That Lost
Its Voice," in the collection *Tales from the South Pacific Islands*
by Ann Gittins. Another version of the story can be found
in James Holding's book *The Sky Eater and Other South Sea
Tales* under the title "The Silent Drum." In developing the
cultural background and learning about Oceanic drumming
traditions, I am indebted to John Kelsey, an ethnomusicologist at Wesleyan University who specializes in the music
of Papua New Guinea, for his help and guidance in referring me to recordings and texts. The staff and secretary at

the Fiji Mission to the United Nations were of tremendous help in sharing materials and in explaining to me many aspects of Fijian culture that relate to the story.

Kim Hyuk-san and the Tiger

This story, under the title "The Father's Legacy," is included in *The Story Bag: A Collection of Korean Folktales*, by Kim So-Un. Under the auspices of the World Music Institute, I was fortunate to be able to meet with Mr. Sang-Won Park, a Korean musician (his main instrument is the *kayagum*, a classical zither) now living in New York City. Mr. Park taught me some basic *changgo* rhythms and generously shared his knowledge about the *changgo* drum, as well as his insights into Korean traditions, philosophy, and music. He also provided the Korean notation for the rhythms included in the story. "Kunbam T'aryông," ("Roasted Chestnuts"), is a traditional Korean song. Children often sing it while playing a game like the choosing game known in North America as "scissors, rock, paper" or "ro-cham-beau." Teacher Eun Kyung Kwon, a native-born Korean who came to this country at the age of seven, discussed the story with me. She allowed me to use her thesis, "A Window into the Korean World View Through Selected Folktales," as part of my research. She generously lent me her family's generational name, Hyuk, for the characters in the story. Sam Solberg also reviewed the story and added valuable insights about Korean music and culture.

Shiva and the Ash-Demon

This story was told to me by Paul Leake in the summer of 1993. Mr. Leake, an American *tabla* player, heard it first from Ustad Masit Khan, the father of his *tabla* teacher,

Ustad Karamat Ullah Khan. Although there are different historical accounts of the origin and development of the *tabla*, this is the myth that was recounted to Paul in 1971 while he stayed in Ustad Masit Khan's house in Calcutta during his studies with the family. Mr. Leake also shared with me a wealth of information on Indian culture, philosophy, and myth gleaned from his own studies and experiences in India, some of which is included in the introduction to the myth. The story was first performed in the United States as a dance piece with the Kathak Ensemble, founded by Paul Leake and dancer Janaki Patric in 1978.

The Legend of the *Bodhran*

This is an original story loosely framed on a motif, found throughout world and European folklore, in which a protagonist spends the night in a haunted house or castle, exorcising the spirits that live there, and receives a reward for doing so. But this story was inspired largely by Christy Barry's depiction of Stevie Mac and the people of County Clare, and of the role of traditional music and *bodhran* playing in their lives. Christy, a flute player, is a native of County Clare currently living in New York City. He has his own group, *Misneach*, which in Gaelic means "courage." In Irish folklore, souls can remain in a state of transit or transformation, which may cause them to appear to the living or to haunt familiar places. I have called this story a legend, but in fact, as far as I know, there are no particular traditions about the origins of using the tipper—the stick—to play the *bodhran*. Even today, some *bodhran* players prefer to play the drum only by hand.

Neima's Rescue

I am indebted to John Bierhorst, a leading scholar and author of works on South and Central American culture and myth, who first introduced this and other source material to me. The retelling for this book is part of a much longer narrative cycle called "Neima and the Evil Spirits," which is included in its original form in the collection *Folk Literature of the Guajiro Indians*, edited by Johannes Wilbert and Karen Simoneau. The story was first transcribed and translated from a Guajiro storyteller by the French anthropologist Michel Perrin, whose classic work *The Way of the Dead Indians: Guajiro Myths and Symbols* was used for research on the *kaashi* drum and Guajiro cultural background.

The Feast for Tepozteco

I first came across this story in the book *The King of the Mountains: A Treasury of Latin American Folk Stories*, by M. A. Jagendorf and R. S. Boggs under the title "The Sacred Drum of Tepozteco." Scholar and author John Bierhorst introduced me to the original Spanish texts included in *Investigación Folklóricá en Mexico*, by Francisco Dominguez; the chapter on Tepoztlán includes two Tepozteco legends. I based my version of the story on these texts. A photo of the rarely seen *teponaztli* drum, the musical notations for its rhythms, and more complete descriptions of La Fiesta de la Virgen de la Natividad are also included in this wonderful source, published by El Instituto Nacional de Bellas Artes in Mexico City.

Miriam at the Red Sea

This is my own version of the Exodus story, and could be called a contemporary *midrash*. A midrash is a legend that expands on or takes as its point of departure verses and stories in the Torah. It is a form of teaching through storytelling that has long been a part of the rabbinic tradition and literature. The figure of Miriam as a musician and dancer occurs in other strands of Jewish folklore as well. See, for example, the title story of Howard Schwartz's collection *Miriam's Tambourine*, which is based on an Eastern European Jewish legend. The part of the story in which Miriam hears a voice telling her not to celebrate the drowning of the Egyptians is drawn from an actual rabbinical midrash that is often found in the Haggadah, the book read at Passover. Through the evidence of archaeological remains such as sculptures and ancient Middle Eastern texts, we know that women did play drums for temple worship and sacred festivals. It is possible that the Biblical character of Miriam was based on someone who played such a role among the ancient Israelites. In preparing this story, I'm grateful to Sabah Nissan, who called my attention to the tradition, in Hebrew, of naming the drum *tof Miriam*, and to ethnomusicologist Dr. Israel Ross for his helpful comments. The *tof* was the first drum I ever played, at the age of seventeen when I was a student at the High School of Music and Art in New York City. It has accompanied me on many journeys. I still have my silver drum, and it is among my most precious possessions.

Epilogue

I am grateful to my friend Mei Mei Sanford, a scholar of Yoruba traditions, woodcarver, and musician, who introduced me to Adeleke Sangoyoyin when he was in New York and with whom she studied when she lived in Nigeria from 1991 to 1992.

Bibliography

⛏ ⛏ ⛏

These are the books and other materials I used in researching the stories and cultural backgrounds for this book.

Adzenyah, Abraham Kobena. "The Acquisition of Musical Knowledge by Traditional Musicians of the Akan Society: A Study of Akan Music Education." Master's thesis, Wesleyan University, 1978.

Appiah, Peggy. *Anansi the Spider: Tales from an Ashanti Village.* New York: Pantheon Books, 1966.

Bierhorst, John. *The Hungry Woman: Myths and Legends of the Aztecs.* New York: William Morrow and Co., 1984.

Bruhac, Joseph and Michael J. Caduto. *Keepers of the Earth: Native American Stories and Environmental Activities for Children.* Golden, CO: Fulcrum Publishing, Inc., 1988.

Cabrera, Lydia. *Anagó: Vocabulario Lucumí.* Miami: Ediciones Universal, 1970.

Canadian Encyclopedia, s.v. "Inuit."

Courlander, Harold. *The Drum and the Hoe: Life and Lore of the Haitian People.* Berkeley: University of California Press, 1960.

———. *The King's Drum and Other African Stories.* New York: Harcourt, Brace and World, 1962.

———. *The Piece of Fire and Other Haitian Tales.* New York: Harcourt, Brace and World, 1964.

Danielou, Alain. *Hindu Polytheism*. London: Routledge and Kegan Paul, 1964.

Deren, Maya. *Divine Horsemen: Voodoo Gods of Haiti*. New York: Dell Books, 1970.

Dominguez, Francisco, et al. *Investigación Folklorica en México Materiales*, vol. 1. Mexico City: Secretaria de Educación Pública Instituto Nacional de Bellas Artes, 1962.

Ekoomiak, Normee. *Arctic Memories*. New York: Henry Holt and Co., 1988.

Fox, Lilla. *Instruments of Religion and Folklore*. New York: Roy Publishers, 1969.

Frishman, Marcia. "Ancient Musical Practice in the Time of the First Temple." Master's thesis, Wesleyan University, 1981.

Gittins, Ann. *Tales from the South Pacific Islands*. Owings Mills, MD: Stemmer House, 1977.

Gourlander, K. A. *An Approach to the Traditional Music of Papua New Guinea*. Papua New Guinea: Goroko Teachers College, 1979.

Hannigan, Steáphán. *The Bodhran Book*. Cork, Ireland: Ossian Publications, Ltd., 1991.

Hartigan, Royal. "Blood Drum Spirit: Drum Languages of West Africa, African-America, Native America, Central Java and South India." Ph.D. dissertation, Wesleyan University, 1986 (available through University Microfilm International).

Holding, James. *The Sky Eater and Other South Sea Tales*. London: Abelard Schuman, 1965.

The Holy Scriptures According to the Masoretic Text. Philadelphia: Jewish Publication Society, 1955.

Jagendorf, M. A., and R. S. Boggs. *The King of the Mountains: A Treasury of Latin American Folk Stories*. New York: Vanguard Press, Inc., 1960.

Johnston, Thomas F., and Tupou Pulu. *Learning Eskimo Drumming*. Anchorage: University of Alaska National Bilingual Materials Development Center.

Kim, So-Un. *The Story Bag: A Collection of Korean Folktales*. Rutland, VT: Charles E. Tuttle Publishing Co., Inc., 1955.

Kinney, Kate. *Pacific Spirits: Pacific Activities Workbook*. Chicago: Field Museum of Natural History, 1990.

Krishnaswamy, S. *Musical Instruments of India*. Boston: Crescendo Publishing Co., 1971.

Kwon, Eun Kyung. "A Window into Korean World View Through Selected Folktales." Master's thesis, Bank Street College of Education, 1993.

Leach, María, ed. *Funk and Wagnall's Standard Dictionary of Folklore, Mythology and Legend*. San Francisco: Harper & Row, 1972.

Lewis, Oscar. *Life in a Mexican Village: Tepoztlán Restudied*. Urbana: University of Illinois Press, 1951.

MacDonald, Margaret Read. *The Storyteller's Source Book*. Detroit: Neal-Schuman Publishers, 1982.

Metayer, Maurice. *Tales from the Igloo*. Edmonton, Alberta: Hurtig Publishers, Ltd., 1972.

Nketia, J. H. Kwabena. *Drumming in Akan Communities of Ghana*. London: Thomas Nelson and Sons, Ltd., 1963.

———. *Our Drums and Drummers*. Accra: Ghana Publishing House, 1968.

Orozco, José Luis. *Cancionero*, vol. 3. Berkeley: Arcoiris Records, 1991.

Perrin, Michel. *The Way of the Dead Indians: Guajiro Myths and Symbols*. Austin: University of Texas Press, 1987.

Polin, Claire. *Music of the Ancient Near East*. Westport, CT: Greenwood Press, 1964.

Redfield, Robert. *Tepoztlán, a Mexican Village: A Study of Folk Life*. Chicago: University of Chicago Press, 1930.

Sendry, Alfred. *Music in Ancient Israel*. New York: Philosophical Library, 1969.

Solberg, S.E. *The Land and People of Korea*. New York: HarperCollins, 1991.

Toor, Frances. *A Treasury of Mexican Folkways*. New York: Crown Publishers, 1964.

Wade, Bonnie C. *Music in India: The Classical Tradition*. New Delhi: Manohar Publications, 1987.

Watson, Lawrence Gray. *Guajiro Personality and Urbanization*. Los Angeles: University of California at Los Angeles, Latin American Center Publications, 1968.

Wilbert, Johannes, and Karen Simoneau, eds. *Folk Literature of the Guajiro Indians*, vol. 2. Los Angeles: University of California at

Los Angeles Latin American Center Publications, 1986.

Wilcken, Lois, with Frisner Augustin. *The Drums of Vodou.* Tempe, AZ: White Cliffs Media Co., 1993.

Yih, Yuen-ming David. "Liturgical Yanvalou Drumming in Port-au-Prince, Haiti." Master's thesis, Wesleyan University, 1988.

Discography

♯ ♯ ♯

Here are some of the recordings I listened to to gain a deeper understanding of the musical traditions represented in this book. Many of these records can be found only in archives or libraries. The Recommended Resources and Publications section of this book will help you find these and other recordings (many of which are now available as tapes and CDs).

Alaskan Eskimo Songs and Stories. University of Washington Press WNA 2765A.

The Boys of the Lough. Trailer Records LER 2086.

A Cry from the Earth: Music of the North American Indians. Edited by John Bierhorst. Folkways FC 7777.

Drums and Chants: Authentic Afro-Cuban Rhythms. Tico LP 1037.

Eskimos of Hudson Bay and Alaska. Recorded by Laura Boulton. Ethnic Folkways Library P 444.

Folk Music of Haiti. Recorded by Harold Courlander. Ethnic Folkways Library. FE 4407.

Indian Drums/Mahapurush Misra, Tabla. Connoisseur Society CM 1466.

Island Music of the South Pacific. Recorded by David Fanshawe. Nonesuch Explorer Series H 72088.

Man's Early Musical Instruments. Curt Sachs. Ethnic Folkways FE 4525.

Music in the World of Islam, vol. 6. Drums and Rhythms. Tangent Records TGS 136.

Papua Niugini: The Iatmul. Of the Music of Oceania series published by the Institute for Musicology of the University of Basle. Musicaphon BM 30SL 2701.

Ravi Shankar: The Sounds of India. Columbia Records PCT 9296.

Traditional Drumming and Dances of Ghana. Folkways Records FC 8858.

World of the South Pacific: Festival of Traditional Music. Musical Heritage Society MHS 3132.

Recommended Resources and Publications

Here are people and places you can call or write to for further information on drumming music from around the world. When needed, I have listed the type of music or information available from the group.

Alaska Native Studies Programs
University of Alaska
508 Gruening
Fairbanks, AK 99775
Inuit

Ali Akbar College of Music
  Store
215 West End Ave.
San Rafael, CA 94901
Indian

Andy's Front Hall
Folk and Traditional Music
P.O. 307
Voorheesville, NY 12186
World

The Asia Society
725 Park Ave.
New York, NY 10021

Bank Street/City Lore Center
  for Folk Arts in Education
Nina Jaffe and Steve Zeitlin,
  codirectors
610 West 112th St.
New York, NY 10025
World music and folklore

Field Museum of Natural
  History
"Pacific Spirits" Exhibit
Roosevelt Rd. at Lakeshore Dr.
Chicago, IL 60605
Pacific Island

Frame Drum Music
Glen Velez, Musician/
  Composer/Researcher
P.O. 955
New York, NY 10024
World

India Currents Magazine
P.O. 21285
San Jose, CA 95151

Latin Music History Archives
Harbor Performing Arts Center
Louis Bauzo, director
1 East 104th St.
New York, NY 10029

Shanachie Records
Dalebrook Park
Ho-Ho-Kus, NJ 07423
Irish and World

Smithsonian Folkways
  Recordings
Smithsonian Institution
Center for Folklife Programs
  and Cultural Studies
955 L'Enfant Plaza, Suite 2600
Washington, DC 20560
World music and folklore

White Cliffs Media Co.—World
  Music Connections
P.O. 433
Tempe, AZ 85280
*World music, especially Caribbean
  and West African*

World Music Archives
Wesleyan University
Middletown, CT 06457

World Music Institute
Robert Browning, Executive
  director
49 West 27th St.
New York, NY 10001

World Music Press
Judith Cook Tucker, publisher
P.O. 2565
Danbury, CT 06813

Further Reading

Blackwood, Alan. *Music: The Illustrated Guide to Music from Around the World from Its Origins to the Present Day.* New York: Mallard Press, 1991.

The Diagram Group. *Musical Instruments of the World: An Illustrated Encyclopedia.* Paddington Press, Ltd., 1976.

Hart, Mickey, and Jay Stevens. *Drumming at the Edge of Magic: A Journey into the Spirit of Percussion.* New York: Harper & Row, 1990.

Marre, Jeremy, and Hannah Charlton. *Beats of the Heart: Popular Music of the World.* New York: Pantheon Books, 1985.

Reck, David. *Music of the Whole Earth.* New York: Charles Scribner's Sons, 1977.

Schwartz, Howard. *Miriam's Tambourine: Jewish Folktales from Around the World.* New York: Oxford University Press, 1988.

Titon, Jeff, ed. *Worlds of Music: An Introduction to the Music of the World's Peoples.* New York: Schirmer Books, 1992.

Wilson, Sule Greg. *The Drummer's Path: Moving the Spirit with Traditional Drumming in Performance and Invocation.* Rochester, VT: Destiny Books, 1992.

About the Author

Nina Jaffe is the coauthor of *While Standing on One Foot, Puzzle Stories and Wisdom Tales from the Jewish Tradition.* A teacher at the Bank Street College of Education, she is codirector of the City Lore/Bank Street Resource Center and is a nationally known storyteller. She lives with her husband and son in New York City.